'TWl

CHARLES FRANCIS KE.   ..1- Trent, England,
in 1848. A man of vast c   .u and multifarious interests, Keary
wrote and published in many genres and on many topics, including
works on Scandinavian mythology, numismatics, religion, history,
and philosophy. He also wrote novels, poetry, verse dramas, and a
handful of stories and sketches in the realm of weird fiction, which
were collected in *'Twixt Dog and Wolf* (1901). This book earned praise
from critics and leading writers of the time such as John Buchan and
Richard Le Gallienne, and Keary's other works won the admiration
of G. K. Chesterton and James Joyce, whose *Dubliners* is thought to
have been influenced by one of Keary's novels. Keary died of heart
failure in 1917.

C. F. KEARY

'TWIXT DOG AND WOLF

Edited with an introduction and notes by
JAMES MACHIN

VALANCOURT BOOKS

Originally published by R. Brimley Johnson, London, 1901
First Valancourt Books edition 2017

This edition © 2017 by Valancourt Books
Introduction and notes © 2017 by James Machin

Published by Valancourt Books, Richmond, Virginia
http://www.valancourtbooks.com

All Valancourt Books publications are printed on acid free paper that
meets all ANSI standards for archival quality paper.

ISBN 978-1-943910-71-7 (paperback)
ISBN 978-1-943910-75-5 (hardcover)
Also available as an electronic book.

Set in Dante MT

INTRODUCTION

'This huge library, growing into unwieldiness, threatening to become a trackless desert of print—how intolerably it weighed upon the spirit!' So despairs a character in *New Grub Street*, George Gissing's celebrated novel of those languishing unsuccessfully at the coalface of literature in the 1880s. The sheer quantity of printed material at the time was the result of a confluence of factors including the cheapening costs of publishing and the expanding literacy of the general public. Inevitably, many unique voices have been almost lost to perpetuity in that 'trackless desert of print', Charles Francis Keary's among them.

Keary was born in 1848, the nephew of the children's author Annie Keary, who had enjoyed considerable success with her 1875 novel *Castle Daly: The Story of an Irish Home Thirty Years Ago*. In its obituary, *The Times* described Keary as a 'novelist' who was 'educated at Marlborough and Trinity College, Cambridge, and was for some years in the Department of Coins at the British Museum.' A Fellow of the Society of Antiquaries, he published non-fictional works on numismatics, history, and comparative mythology, before turning his hand to what the *Bookman* described as 'lighter literature' after ending his tenure at the British Museum. He also produced travelogues, including a semi-fictional work called *The Wanderer* (1888), which appeared under the rather splendid pseudonym H. Ogram Matuce. That he was a typical late-Victorian polymath is suggested by the titles of just two of his books from the early 1890s: *The Vikings in Western Christendom A.D. 789 to A.D. 888* (1891) and *A Mariage de Convenance* (1893). Among his friends was the composer Frederick Delius, for whom he had discussed producing a libretto for an opera, a project which never came to fruition. The poet and critic John Bailey refers to Keary 'already being an invalid' by the time Bailey became acquainted with him in 1916, the year before his death at the age of 69. The *Spink Numismatic Circular* gives his address at this time as 5 Cambridge Terrace, Hyde Park, London.

The *Times* obituary said of Keary's novels that they aim 'at depicting life, after the manner of the great Russian writers, in its chaotic reality and avoiding conventional selection and arrangement', adding that while they 'never had a large popular circulation' they were 'very highly thought of within the limited literary set'. By the 1890s, the *Bookman* also regarded Keary as a 'diligent contributor to periodical literature', listing among the venues for his stories the *Contemporary*, *Nineteenth Century*, *Mind*, *Macmillan's Magazine*, the *National Review*, *Saturday Review*, *Athenæum*, and the *St. James's Gazette*. It is from the pages of such magazines that much of the content of *'Twixt Dog and Wolf* was compiled.

The stories which constitute *'Twixt Dog and Wolf* are of distinct contrast to his novels, the latter being exercises in what the *Speaker* described as 'the modern political and social sphere' of fiction. The title comes from the French expression for twilight, *'Entre chien et loup'*, which conveys so poetically the eerie crepuscular shift from the prosaic and familiar to the baleful and unknown. *'Twixt Dog and Wolf* collects work that is unmistakably tinged with the yellow hue of the era, and expertly evokes an oneiric, vesperal realm of disconcerting shadows and dark forces moving unseen, yet tangible, in tandem with our own.

Both John Buchan and Richard Le Gallienne were voluble in their praise in their reader's reports for the collection of short stories and sketches first submitted by Keary to John Lane in 1897 under the title *'Twixt Dog and Wolf*. At least some of the contents of the collection were already familiar to both since they had already recently appeared in the *New Review* (under W. E. Henley's editorship) and *Macmillan's*. Buchan had 'read some of them in the *New Review* and admired them greatly' while Le Gallienne knew of Keary at least by reputation: 'I happen to know that Mr Henley thought ["Elizabeth"] an extraordinarily fine piece of work.' As well as short stories, the volume contained some prose poems or fables ('Phantasies'), of which Le Gallienne opined, 'some are very pretty and quasi-symbolical, some are weird and horrible—all are worth reprinting.' He continued:

> I do not think you need have any hesitation in publishing this book. It is a collection of stories—in the case of 'Phantasies' of course something slighter—each with an element of the weird, the uncanny, the mystical. Such an element, well managed, will always attract readers, and Mr. Keary's management of it is one of the best I have ever seen.

Buchan's endorsement of *'Twixt Dog and Wolf* was similarly effusive:

> He writes carefully and exquisitely, without the vice of artifice which spoils so much of modern work. His sketches are stories of *diablerie* of the strange sights and sounds which follow on the twilight, between the dog barking and the appearance of the grey wolf. The first is a tale of the conflict between the ordinary Greek religion and the old wild nature worship—of Pan and the nymphs—which it displaced. The second *Elizabeth* is a story of medieval Germany—one of the finest witch-tales I know. The *Four Students* is a tale of the Paris of the Revolution. *Phantasies* are slightly different: I am not sure that I always catch Keary's meaning; but they seem to me in the whole to be nearly as good work in metaphysics as Stevenson's *Fables*.
>
> Mr Keary has wide knowledge, a great gift of style, and a wonderful power of suggesting vague mystery. His work is in every way admirable and I gladly recommend you to take the book.

Despite their enthusiasm, the book was not published by John Lane, who perhaps was still too chary after the Wilde trial to involve himself with material that exuded the pungent, and now tainted, aroma of decadence. *'Twixt Dog and Wolf* did not in fact see publication until 1901. It received mention in Keary's

Times obituary as 'a series of short sketches in the weird and *macabre* […] excellently done.'

The contents of *'Twixt Dog and Wolf* are not immediately resolvable into a coherent theme, but are rather each distinct in their foray into this 'weird and *macabre*' territory. 'The Message from the God' may remind the reader of Heinrich Heine's 'Gods in Exile' (1854) or Pater's *Marius the Epicurian* (1885), and has numerous analogues among the myriad cultural expressions of the late nineteenth century enthusiasm for Pan-worship and classical paganism.

'Elizabeth' is the longest story in the collection, originally published in two parts in the *New Review* in 1896. It is unmistakably informed by the early nineteenth century German Romanticism of Joseph von Eichendorff, and the full subtleties of its imagery may perhaps only be parsed by someone with a thorough grounding in alchemical allegory and symbolism. It shares with 'The Four Students' a beautifully executed elision of the rational with the subconscious; the mundane world being ineluctably superseded by shadowy chthonic forces. In the latter tale, Keary starkly evokes the queasy paranoia of the Terror and conjures a chilling geographical association between the site of the Jacobins' mass executions and that of the hideous rites of antique pagan ritual, suggesting that the influence of the same maleficent *genius loci* is responsible for both.

Keary's series of 'Phantasies', some of which could be described as prose poems, share a similar, inexorable dream logic, suggestive of Marcel Schwob's shorter sketches, with which Keary may well have been familiar. Despite the accuracy of Buchan's comparison to Stevenson's *Fables* above, they all have a sinister implication of a nebulous angst usually lacking in Stevenson's rather jauntier affairs, although both share the same sardonic edge.

The question remains whether Keary's failure to find enduring traction as a writer was a result of this new abundance of competition or his own limitations. While recognising Keary's facility as a writer, Bailey thought that Keary 'had neither the power which compels recognition nor the assured faith which can go on confidently without it.' G. K. Chesterton was less equivocal in his praise, remarking of *The Wanderer* that of 'the singularly beautiful style in which the book is written it is unnecessary, to any reader of Mr. Keary, to speak.' Another admirer was James Joyce, who mentions Keary in a 1905 letter to his brother Stanislaus, and perhaps took inspiration for *Dubliners* from Keary's 1905 novel of variegated London life *Bloomsbury*. The *Academy* went so far as to laud Keary as one whose failures were 'more interesting than the successes of most people'.

Keary's writing, therefore, was not short of admirers. Bailey remarked that Keary 'might, perhaps, have been greater if fate had been kinder', going on to say, perspicaciously, that 'there is in most of his work a suggestion of disappointment and heaviness of spirit, of a journey which is always uphill.' Indeed, one can certainly find an ubiquitous sense of underlying pessimism throughout the pages of *'Twixt Dog and Wolf.* However, as Chesterton suggests, Keary's mastery of style means that the writing is never overburdened by the gloom of its subject matter. Rather, Keary's accomplishment is such that these stories and sketches delight and entertain, even as they contemplate some vague and dismal abyss.

JAMES MACHIN

JAMES MACHIN is a London-based scholar with an interest in weird and supernatural fiction, especially of the Victorian and Edwardian eras. He is co-editor of *Faunus*, the journal of the Friends of Arthur Machen.

The extracts from the John Lane readers' reports are used by kind permission of the Harry Ransom Center at the University of Texas, Austin. James Machin would like to thank the Center, as well as the Creekmore and Adele Fath Charitable Foundation and the University of Texas at Austin Office of Graduate Studies for supporting his visiting fellowship in 2014. He would also like to thank Joseph Brooker, Lionel Carley, and Bernard McGinley for their help in finding information about Keary.

Entre Chien et Loup

A dog is howling at the court-yard door;
Within, the horses drag their halter-chains;
Behold! the world is full of misty rains;
And the old Shepherd knows the twilight frore.*
The sea of Night will soon the Vale engulf,
With waves of dimness washing to the height;
And now from a near pinewood into sight
Steals one grey wolf.

CONTENTS

AS BREATH INTO THE WIND

PHANTASIES

I

THE MESSAGE FROM THE GOD

'BUT what did the Thracian soothsayer command you to do?' said Lysias.

'That,' answered Glaucon, 'I am forbidden to say.'

'Some act of worship, I doubt not,' rejoined the other, 'and in behalf of the gods, not on thine own behalf. For ever wast thou the most pious of men.'

But he spoke half mockingly.

'What we do for the gods we do for ourselves,' said the young priest with gravity.

And he looked up at the temple beside them. It rose above its platform, the steps of which bathed their feet in the blue sea. Behind nodded the dark pine-trees in the *temenos*★ of the god, and on the other hand Titanus flowed hardly among its reeds and lost itself in the salt water.

But Lysias answered him.

'Ourselves? What can we do for ourselves?' he cried. 'See here, Glaucon! Are we not Hellenes, you and I? You boast, I know, that on this shore your ancestors stood. How many thousands of brazen Greeks have marched since then into this land, and through it into farther Asia, and from Asia to Egypt or beyond the Hydaspes itself? Whence do we come now? Even from bearing arms, not for ourselves but for the Romans, in far Germany. Vain ambitions! vain attempts! only to flatter the vanity of Cæsar. For who will ever subdue those intraversable forests, those dark meres?'

'Not so,' replied his companion. 'The gods are Greece; the Romans are but their hoplites. See here,' and therewith he extended his arm to where the coast stretched its long line of bays and promontories, each headland crowned by its marble temple. Already they were growing golden and misty in the westering sunlight. 'That tongue of land away southward is the Hydra promontory. There, according to our tradition, Heracles slew the serpent. Thence, too, he embarked on his last voyage, when he left Lycia and turned his face to Trachis.'

'Such was the doom dispensed by Zeus,' said Lysias, quoting from the tragedian.

'The flames bore him to heaven,' continued Glaucon solemnly, 'and he became a god. Is he not honoured now by all men over the whole earth? By the fierce Tyrians, away southward—yea, I have heard by man-eating Libyans beyond Atlas, close to the torrid zone; not less by the savage Marcomanni* whom we saw dancing their naked sword-dance in the depths of their woods, and sounding their melancholy horns.'

'Zeus!' said Lysias. 'I have served in too many lands and under too many gods.'

'There are no gods but ours,' reiterated Glaucon.

And at that moment a whisper came from the reeds beside them, and a certain fear fell upon the speaker.

'There have been other gods,' his companion replied. 'Here I have heard that, many ages before your Apollo had his temple, Titanus was a god, whom Pan begot by the nymph Æglê. Now some only of the shepherds pay their vows to him; yet whether men bring him sacrifices or no, he cares not at all, neither he nor his nymphs. But they play still among the reeds here, where the fresh water runs into the sea. Only our sight is dimmed, so that we can no longer see them. And if your temple should crumble into dust, as, indeed, it is no longer fresh and new as it was at the prime—for I doubt there be not such large offerings to Gryneian Apollo* as once there were—yet will the river-god continue there to disport him in the soft water. Unto thee, then, old Titanus,' he cried, turning his back upon the temple and his face to the rushes, 'I vow a spotless kid three days hence at the new moon'; and as he said this Lysias laughed.

But Glaucon shuddered, for he knew, by the prophecy of the Thracian, that Lysias had spoken an ill-omened word. But the other, still laughing, took his way up the river-bank, and was soon lost to sight behind the headland and the grove. Then Glaucon turned about and ascended to the temple to perform the rites.

II

And when all that had been commanded him had been duly done, the young priest came out of the shrine, and, standing with his face westward, looked over the Ægean. He held his hands stretched out before him, and stood there motionless awhile as if he prayed.

'Speak to me, even to me,' he whispered, 'O son of Golden Hope, immortal *Voice*.'

Silently, the while, marble Gryneia looked down upon the waves which fawned at her feet. Now a little higher up, now a hand's-breadth farther down, they kept on their low monotonous murmur about those temple steps. From beneath the eaves, from along the peristyle, came back a whispering echo. The sparrows chattered in their turn from the roof or among the figures on the pediment.

'O immeasurable world!' mused the Greek. 'O grandeur of Greece! O might of Apollo!'

Upon this shore, as Lysias had said, had his ancestors fallen, ages ago, when the Argives first set foot in Asia. Even then Gryneian Apollo had lorded it in his temple, and was worshipped by Greeks and Trojans alike. Through all the centuries since then the marble face of his dwelling had looked westward, and had flamed crimson each evening when the sun set in the purple sea. Now, as the young priest said once more to himself—now all the nations worshipped the gods of Greece: the Romans first, thither in the West, and through the Romans countless other races onward to the end of the world, where the gates of Heracles led the way to untraversed

Ocean, Amphitrite's wide chamber, and to lands not of mortal men.

Glaucon stood there, a solitary figure facing the sunset. For generations his family had furnished the priesthood of Apollo's shrine. He now was the last of his race. Yet this was scarce a thing to grieve over, for only on such a condition could the prophecy of the Thracian be fulfilled, the message from the god delivered.

It was true what Lysias had hinted. Not such crowds as of old came there to worship or brought gifts. Fewer still ever stayed near the temple after sunset, or entered the pine-tree enclosure at nightfall; for there the shepherds on the high downs declared they had beheld white presences like unto wreaths of mist float among the upper branches of the trees. These were, they said, the spirits of human victims—of those who, through the ages, had been sacrificed to the god at his yearly feast of atonement, or in some great purification when sickness devastated the country.

Helios touched upon the Western Sea. What had been like a bank of cloud grew suddenly solid. It was the Island of Lesbos. A great streak as of blood marked the Hydra promontory. The cliff put on that crimson stain each evening because at that hour had leapt up the flames of the hero's funeral pyre on Mount Œta—the flames, as Glaucon had said just now, that bore him to heaven.

The young priest was but newly returned from service in the Macedonian legion and in the army of Domitius Ahenobarbus. Under that General the Romans had penetrated further than their arms had ever before reached into the territory of the Germans. He had lately lost a brother quartered at Aliso, fallen among the Cherusci, fierce and cunning.

In all these lands he had found his gods reverenced even by men who did not respect the might of Cæsar. Yea, far as the world extended on every side—Tyrians and Turones, Scythians and Sigambri, Gauls and Goths—men worshipped the gods of Greece.

'At this moment,' the young legionary said to himself, 'the camp-fires are being lighted along the Roman lines. The Germans are driving their cattle home by the swampy woodland paths. Their small houses shine white through the dusk, and unnumbered cranes rise from the dim marshes and wheel on high uttering their doleful chorus.'

An awe fell upon his soul, for, as if in answer to his thought, behold there came out of the sunset, black against its crimson, a marshalled flight of swans winging straight towards him in a long line. The clang of their wings was like the clash of arms in the distance. This must indeed be the first token from the god. Now of a sudden they changed front, the whole line shook, then it reformed. Alas! it turned further to the south, and passed him on the *left* hand. And trouble smote the heart of the watcher.

As he stood musing, the sun went down, and a wind passed by, and with the wind the reeds began once again to shake their heads and whisper.

'Before this temple was . . .' they murmured.

Glaucon would not listen. Was it indeed an outward voice or the thought which Lysias had imparted that leapt once more into his mind? The after-glow had nearly gone. Night, rising from the east, was spreading wide her sombre mantle. Yet, though her garment floated from her, it was not possible to read the expression on her shaded face. Glaucon turned his eyes towards her countenance and his back upon the sea. Every moment she drew nearer, yet none could hear her tread. The waves and the sparrows had alike ceased talking, and through the Greek's mind, though he had for a moment forgotten where he was or why, reverberated the dreadful echo of the Soothsayer's prophecy, his message of hope and fear.

Now the marble temple looked like a wraith. Still there came the murmur of the reeds.

'Before this temple was . . .'

Before! Who had reigned here when nought but the bare

slope rose above the sea, when even the grove of Apollo was unplanted? Even then the reeds had grown in the river, and among the reeds had sported the nymphs, and with the nymphs had played great Pan himself.

And Glaucon shuddered and was afraid. Images of death began to rise in his mind, of pale ghosts and spiritless *lemures.** He no longer saw the conquering arms of the Romans or heard the tread of their legionaries up the rocky passes. Rather he beheld the wild-eyed Germans and their vast marshes black as those of Styx, over which travelled fatuous wandering lights. Or, again, he saw that dreadful island of which he had once beheld the faint outline opposite the coast of Gaul, whither it was said the *coloni** on the Gaulish coast had laid upon them the task of ferrying over the dead—the dead who journeyed thither from all known lands. At depth of night to each fisherman in rotation there came a knock upon his door and a whispering breath summoning him to the beach. There he found his boat got ready for a voyage, empty to mortal eyes, yet weighed down as if by a heavy freight. And the mariner set sail and carried his unseen burden to the island in the sea, whence voices could be heard and people answering as if in rotation till the boat again grew light.

Such were the thoughts of Glaucon, for of a truth Pan or another had touched his cheek.

Now he had wandered unwittingly into the grove. Surely he deemed he could hear a light sound of muttering ghosts. The dark branches swayed and groaned above his head. A cold terror lay upon his limbs and rooted him to the earth, and lifted the hair upon his head, while all the time he could hear the murmur of the rushes by the river, now quite audible.

'Before men worshipped Zeus or Apollo they worshipped him, mighty Pan.'

Yet there was worse to come. He tried not to listen. A chilly wind blew through him, and panic fear rested upon his soul. Shrilly muttered the ghosts in the trees. At last the branches parted to show him the great sweep of the river, not half empty as he knew it, but in full flood—a sheet of slate-coloured water, and along by the edge of the stream moved a great company.

'If we had eyes to see,' Lysias had said.

Glaucon's eyes were opened, and he did see—a great company, satyrs girt with sedge, nymphs with dark weeds in their tresses, whose hair yet hung down in dank masses; a wailing dirge rose from their lips. Now came in view the end of the procession; they were carrying the Great God himself. He was pale as a corpse.

'Worshipped mighty Pan,' the reeds whispered again, 'and now Great Pan is dead.'

Unspeakable terror! A light was moving towards him among the trees. When it drew nearer he saw that in the light was framed a face, pale, too, but not lifeless, haggard, with long hair, the colour of wine, falling upon his shoulders—a face at once severe and mild. Upon the forehead there were drops of blood, and about the wine-coloured locks a dusky crown.

Glaucon burst from the enclosure, and ran he knew not whither. All along the shore of the Ægean he went. And now the wind was rising, the sky was overcast, the promontories were hidden by clouds. Beneath his feet, as he hurried on, the rushes and the waves sent up the same fearful murmur, which anon swelled into a mighty voice, and the voice sped before him proclaiming:

'Great Pan is dead.'

And people lying awake that night by casements overlooking the dark sea heard the same tone, which ran along the coast of the Ægean, and always the word was:

'Great Pan is dead.'

II

ELIZABETH

'What is this place?
                    A place inhabitable.
The dreadful maids, daughters of Earth and Gloom
    Possess it.'—Œdip. Col.*

I

ELIZABETH hastened her steps. She did so by instinct so long as Rettenberg Castle remained in sight, and consciously or unconsciously breathed a sigh of relief so soon as she had passed the elbow which shut in her own Valley of the Lehen. Now she had her back upon the Mosel, her face looking up the valley to the west. The flat watered meadows at her right had put on their darkest green, and in the high woods upon the other hand night had already set her foot. Over the castle there had hung a half moon. But the friendly planet travelled with her, and now looked down through the black branches of the trees. The yellow glow of sunset was still before her face. The woman passed on, fearing no ill.

Of a sudden from out of the wood floated a single point of light. It rose, then sank as if to anchor upon a wild briar beside the path, then mounted again, hung for one instant suspense against the orange sky, and disappeared. Elizabeth crossed herself. Once in her life, while she was yet a child, had she seen such a vision. Yet these fairy tapers were known to all men by tradition: they were the candles of the elves, those beings who had lived and lorded it ages ago as kings of the mountains and the valleys, until Christ the Lord came, and drove them away. They were deposed, but not destroyed: they lived on, and now kept vast treasures hidden in caves and beneath rivers; and it was said that to men who feared them not. . . .

Elizabeth had bent down her head when she saw the light; and crossed herself. She thought that at that moment it disappeared; at the same instant she heard faint and very far off a single bell from St. Boniface's minster at Andersbach, which lay just so far below Lehndorf that Rettenberg stood above it.

But now another and another minute flame sailed out of the wood. A vision passed before the peasant woman's mind of the great minster church, of the priests walking therein carrying tapers. She could no longer keep her eyes closed. The elves' candles crossed and re-crossed her path, rose, descended, went out, lighted themselves again. Nay, it was not possible to feel afraid at heart, nor hate these heathen fairies as they ought to be feared and hated; not even as she feared the Freyherr's men, and hated the sight of Rettenberg.

The village houses nodded friendly welcome. They stood scattered at irregular heights on the slightly rising ground, their brown faces and brown-thatched roofs beginning to grow together in the gathering gloom. On one flat space stood the village fountain. Only crazy Jutta remained near the splashing water, which had been surrounded by gossips half an hour earlier, and was even now repeating inarticulately the chattering talk to which it had been a listener.

'Tu-whoo, tu-whoo,' cried old Jutta. 'Go and find wicked Hilda, Elizabeth of the Out-born. Then shalt thou come to thine own. But better come and live in the village, Elizabeth of the Corner.' And now she changed her cry, and began to imitate the screech-owl.

There were some indeed who said that Carl's cottage, Elizabeth's husband's, lay not truly within the village boundary, or had not always been within it—inside, that is, the circle traced by the priest when thrice a year he went round the parish, and read a passage of Scripture at each of the gospel oaks, and the prayers against evil spirits which keep in air, whence are all kinds of pestilence, and diseases, and sickness, that they may be driven out and the air made pure and clean. It was a mere tale this concerning their house, 'The Corner,' a story of old days not worth thinking on. Priest Gebhard must have blessed their land a score of times by now. Yet this night Elizabeth shuddered for the first time at Jutta's words.

II

Friendly and most pleasant was the shelter of her own dim roof, was the breath of her own kine* beneath it, of Tecla, the six-year-old cow, who had her calf at her side. Elizabeth heard and smelt before she saw them. When she had kindled her fire to prepare the supper the flames changed lights and shadows on the walls and in the pitched roof, and sent up fitful gleams into the gallery at one end, reached by a ladder wherein was her bed, hers and Carl's. Beyond the passage they shone upon the nose and horns of Tecla, who turned her head and looked encouragingly and kindly down upon her mistress as she bent over her pot.

Had not the cow lowed directly Elizabeth set foot within the door? It was a good sign! Yet Carl still delayed. Now she heard his step—from the side of the forest: would it had been from the other side. He was carrying something, too—she could tell that from his walk. In spite of herself Elizabeth gave a shiver, and did not look round the moment her husband lifted the latch. The fire upon the low hearth glowed dull red under the iron pot, and did not reach the figure of the man, who passed first into the cattle-stall before he came and sat himself down in the room—a thick-set man, with matted fair hair and red beard. Elizabeth was darker, with deep-seated eyes.

'Good e'en.' No other greeting passed between husband and wife. They drew their stools in silence to the hearth, and Elizabeth poured out the supper. But all the while Carl's grey eyes were bright, and restless, and eager. When he had eaten, his tongue was loosed. 'I have seen strange sights,' he began, and then hesitated. His wife did not speak, but her eye searched his face in the firelight.

'I was with young Willebald in the forest,' he went on; 'and we were—in faith we were digging for pig-roots. And anon Willebald grew so sleepy that he was fain to lie down. And he had his head against my foot. And I vow to you that, as he lay there, a little beast like to a snake came out of his mouth, and it got you upon the grass, and wriggled itself away an arm's length about, till it came to the edge of the brook by which we were. And behold! I could not stir for wonder. But at the brook the little thing stayed, as if it were minded to pass over, but could not. Nay, it moved up and down at the edge of the water, as if it were seeking how to cross. Then at last I took my spear——'

'O Carl,' cried Elizabeth, 'you carried a spear to dig for roots? And it is forbidden, thou knowest.'

'Ay, ay,' he answered in a gruff voice. But presently he went on with his tale:—'And when I had laid my spear across the stream, the little beast like a snake, behold! it wriggled me across by the spear, and went away on the other side, and then it passed out of sight into a manner of cleft or cave under the rock.' Carl stopped here suddenly in his story.

'It is an enchantment! Some ill is coming upon him!' cried Elizabeth in deep distress, but rather as if speaking to herself. 'And the lanterns of the elves? What should they signify?'

'Nay, nay, listen,' Carl answered testily. 'Anon it comes me back again, and it crossed the spear, even as it had done before, only backwise—seest thou?—and then, behold! he slipped him into Willebald's mouth again, whence he had come. What think you of that?' Carl was wide-eyed and open-mouthed. Elizabeth could answer nothing but a long-drawn 'O!' Then he went on. 'What thinkest thou of this? Willebald he wakes, and says, "Comrade," he saith, "I dreamt the strangest of dreams, sure, that any man ever had. For me seemed I crossed a river upon a great round bridge, which was of iron at one end. And I wandered in a forest, till I came to a mighty great cave, and

at the end thereof was a pit." '—('O Jesu!' breathed again from
the wife almost inaudibly)—' "And at the bottom of the pit
was another mighty great cavern, great as the minster church
at Andersbach, and therein were many men that walked and
carried great jewels in their heads; and they shone," said Willebald, "like sparks of flame." '

'Like sparks of flame!'

'But I said,' Carl went on, ' "Comrade, thou art certainly
damned, and I too maybe, if we stay here." And then I told
him what I had seen. Now, behold! Willebald is a stout-hearted
man, and not as other men, nay, and he is but a youth and over
rash. For when I told him my vision, I said that for sure the
Devil was in this place, and we must run away; and I ran. But
he came after, crying:—"No!" and that I should stay and show
him the place where the little beast had entered into the rock;
for that there surely we should find the treasure of jewels that
he had seen in his sleep. But I withstood him, and would by no
means stay, and was minded only to run away from that place.
Yet now, forsooth, I almost think——'

'O, no. It was well. Thou didst well,' Elizabeth cried with
fervour.

'Nay, now I am at home,' Carl went on, at once taking the
opposite side from his wife, 'I am minded to think——'

'Carl,' said Elizabeth, earnestly laying her hand upon his
arm, 'go not again—take not Willebald again into the forest.
He is too bold. This evening I have seen——'

But she never finished her sentence. For it was then that the
two Foresters came into the cottage.

III

The latch opened, while she was speaking, and a mocking
voice said: 'Carl, take not Willebald into the forest!'

Both the man and his wife started from their seats. A laugh
came from the person who had spoken, and who was now in
the room. At the same moment his comrade followed him.

The dress of the two admitted of no doubt as to their occupation: they were two of the Freyherr's rangers. They wore jerkins, caps, and hose, all of untanned hide. Each had a boar-spear in his hand, but a spear, as Carl could not but note, of old-fashioned make; and they had long-bows at their backs. And that too, thought Carl, is strange. For all the other foresters carried cross-bows. They gave their names as Gotschalk and Rudolf.

Though he now sat still, the peasant's eyes glittered, not in a friendly way. By the villagers the lord's men were dreaded and disliked, and yet welcomed for the sake of the news they brought—news of the castle, and thereby intelligence of a still wider world. As for Elizabeth, her thoughts were so haunted that evening by a fear of the supernatural that it was a pleasure to see creatures of flesh and blood. She got up to prepare a fresh supper of cabbage soup and porridge, and passed out of the firelight.

The peasant and his wife had been seated upon two stools, the only ones the room contained. But along one end of the chamber and half way down another wall ran two settles, and it was on the nearer of these that the new-comers placed themselves. The glow of the embers hardly reached them. With a peasant's caution, Carl forbore to begin a conversation, and at first the rangers seemed no more talkative than he. So for a while the company sat in silence and semi-darkness.

'Ay,' at last said Gotschalk to his comrade. 'We are in luck to find Carl of the Corner not yet gone to roost, eh, Rudolf? We are weary,' he went on to his host. 'We have been all day a-hunting.' 'Ay, a-hunting,' said the second ranger, and he gave a low guttural laugh, which seemed to Elizabeth, returning to the room at that moment, to jar her very spine.

Presently Carl was asking them concerning a rumour which had reached the village: that the Freyherr was among his men, as if for war. And 'O,' said Gotschalk, with high contempt, 'Lord Otto is half a monk. He will never know from what side danger comes.' And 'No,' said Rudolf, 'he will never see the Red Spectre till it is at his door.'

If a thunderbolt had fallen the cottage folk could hardly have been more astounded. Everybody knew what sort of punishment talk of that sort from a lord's servant might bring down. And for these two rangers to put themselves even in danger from unknown peasants was beyond reason rash. Yet they seemed perfectly indifferent. And soon a still stranger thing happened. For Rudolf, seeing Elizabeth place the pot over the fire, picked up something from beside him and said: 'Here is something better than cabbage to put in your pot.'

He held up his prize in the firelight. It was a large grey hare. Carl sprang from his stool, and grasped his knife. Just such a hare had he brought home that evening, and hidden among the bean-stalks above the cow-stall. For a moment he supposed that the game-keeper had unearthed his game. But he recovered himself, and sat down once more with wary eyes. 'You take the Freyherr's game?' he said. 'O,' said Rudolf, with another of his grating laughs, 'Lord Otto'—(Elizabeth noted and remembered afterwards how they always spoke of the Freyherr as Lord Otto)—'is open-handed. He never hunts in the place where this was found, and gives good leave to whoso will to help himself.'

'Whoso of his rangers?' said Carl. 'Nay, whoso will,' said Gotschalk. 'Yet none but a forester born,' his comrade went on. 'Born or unborn,' put in Gotschalk: whereat they both laughed, though what might be the reason of the interruption the others could not guess.

'None but a forester born—with eyes that see in the dark— could have found this hare.' And, indeed, his eyes shone in the half light like the eyes of a ferret, fiery and red.

'Dark in this moonlight?' Elizabeth queried, surprised into speaking. For even now from the chimney-hole under the roof the moon made a patch of blue light upon the smoke where it entered the cowl. 'Why, where could that have been?'

'Dark as pitch,' said Gotschalk, 'on the common by the Three Pines.'

Carl and his wife did not stay to ask how it could possibly be without a moon upon that windy heath. A more moving thought possessed them. 'The Three Pines!' they exclaimed with one voice. 'Why, that is in Hilda's Land!'

And the shudder which passed down Elizabeth's back now almost sharpened itself into a scream. For at that very moment a screech-owl glided past their door, and uttered its dismal sound, the Wicked Hilda's cry.

IV

Blood was in all men's thoughts. Henry with the Scar had been in the village but half an hour ago, and, standing by the fountain, had related how, when he and William Peterson were on guard upon the castle battlements only two nights agone, they had beheld, proceeding from the eastern heavens, a great army, with lances set and pennons flying, which marched as it were up the sky. Next, turning westward, they saw another army of like aspect move up to meet the first. And the two hosts encountered in mid-heaven. Henry and William saw the spears engage and break, nay, men and horses go down, in the shock, until at last the eastern army overcame the western, and drove it away over the horizon; and awhile the sky remained as clear as if it were a frosty winter's night. Then, just as they were wondering what this vision might portend, behold the centre of heaven was suffused by a great stream of blood, which again ran out sideways in separate rivulets, and anon this vision also passed.

It was thus that Henry with the Scar had told his tale by the fountain, and, old halberdier that he was, his face was pale and scared. Now, though it was only the sunset which dyed the water of the fountain, people thought they saw blood in it too. They strained their eyes in the direction to which Henry had pointed as that whence the first army came.

'Yes: I deem Blankenroth lies that way,' one of the older peasants acknowledged when they appealed to him. For every one knew that the curse upon the castle, Hilda's curse, would some day be fulfilled, and that a host was destined to march from Blankenroth against the Lord of Rettenberg. Hilda the witch would ride with the army, and the Red Spectre was to lead it. But who was the Red Spectre not many knew, not many liked to ask.

Elizabeth had listened to this talk, but without much heeding, her mind being occupied by private cares. She left the tank, and passed up beside their field, where a hoe had not fallen for many a day, and the weeds were growing high. What could she do alone? It was business enough to look after Tecla and her calf, to take them out by day, to browse on the edge of the wood, and bring them home at evening: to milk the cow, and pour the milk into the clay holes in the ground, and cover it with straw and dung for cheese-making. How could she work in the fields as well? And Carl, who ought to have seen to this, where was he? Ever since the day when the Two Foresters came to the cottage, Carl had neglected his fields, and spent his time a-hunting in the forest—Was it even in the forest? Or on the moor? Elizabeth never dared to ask where he spent his time, nor to think of the risks they ran—he, Carl, and that other one. Did Carl and *he* hunt along with the two rangers? Were the Lord's men only luring them on to discovery and punishment? These things would not bear thinking on. They always had meat in their pot o' nights now, when her husband was at home. But Elizabeth ate it trembling, and longed for the old days of porridge and cabbage-soup.

To-night, as she toiled up the steep little path which led to their outlying cottage, she felt too weary and heart-sick for words. She had to go into the house and shake down the dried ferns for Tecla's bed. She found some cold remnant of the midday's meal, and brought it out to eat at the forest door—for one door faced toward the village and one toward the wood— sitting there always and waiting (as she said to herself) for her husband. The evening was warm enough; the stars were coming out one by one, but there was no moon. A certain thought oppressed her more than it had ever done before. It was that question which was now and again debated in the village, which had given rise not long since to taunts from crazy Jutta: the doubt whether their house was by right in either Lehndorf of Rittenberg or Abbot's Lehndorf, and had not been built upon a strip stolen from that No-man's Land which belonged to neither, but was left wild and desolate, with the rest of it thick wood or mere uncultivated heath, which even travellers did not willingly cross—and was known from old traditions as Hilda's Land. And as she thought these thoughts, Elizabeth heard, as she had done that night when the foresters came to the house, the cry of the screech-owl*—Hilda's cry. It was not near this time, but away in the wood. It curdled the blood in her veins. She longed now to shut herself indoors and light a fire to comfort her. But she felt rooted where she sat, as if she were condemned to wait and wait while the cry should come nearer and nearer, until. . . .

Some cloud must have spread over the sky or some mist have arisen from the earth, for it grew pitch dark. And now another noise, a strange one at this time of night, smote upon her ear—the baying of hounds: not near this either, but away off. The voices echoed far in the woody distance.

Some time thus passed. Of a sudden, without a word or a touch, two figures went by her. She knew them instinctively for her husband and Willebald. They had passed her seat, they had rushed into the house; and *something* was in pursuit of them. This too she knew: yet how? She had felt nothing nor heard so much as the sound of a footfall.

'Willebald, speak! what is it?' she cried in terror. No answer came; unless indeed it were that she was answered by a growl.

She followed into the house, crying all the while on Carl and Willebald. But none spoke. Then something ran against her; she fell over it, and felt the shaggy coat of a hound. She fell forwards, and, as her hand touched the floor, she found it all wet, a sticky moistness that she knew well for blood.

During one half second she realised this. But in falling she struck her head against the corner of the hearthstone, and a blanket of oblivion fell around her.

V

What cries of mourning were these? what deep wailings as from subterraneous depths, then shot with metallic sounds as of trumpets? There was one order of visions never very far from the mind of Elizabeth, as of any imaginative peasant of those days: these were visions of the under-world, of the devils and the wailing dead, or, again, of the Judgment Day and its awful Trump. Had she then died that moment since, when she felt the blood and struck her head. But, as Elizabeth came more and more to herself, the sounds contracted and lessened, until they became nothing more than the deep low of Tecla and the lighter one of the calf beside her—these, with the crying of cocks in the village! Grey dawn was stealing into the room. Elizabeth looked down, expecting to see the floor all stained with blood. There was nothing; her hands, too, were clean of all trace of it. And, greatest wonder of all, there was Carl seated by the hearthstone, eating his breakfast—no less. The woman sprang up and embraced her husband, a thing not common between them. Carl took it somewhat grumpily. How strange, Elizabeth thought afterwards, that he should have sat by while she lay stretched out upon the earth! But had she really lain there? More and more, as the minutes flew by, the whole thing took for her the shape of a fantastic dream.

They dined richly that night. Carl, for his part, seemed to have put away all fear, and, for the first time, Elizabeth shared some of the same feeling. She was growing used to the state of things. It seemed ages ago now since she first began to tremble when from time to time her husband brought home a head of game to plenish their larder. Notwithstanding, she noted first at this meal how greatly her husband was changed. Had he indeed put away all fear? Certainly, he was no longer the timid, cautious man she had known only a month ago. But why did he seem to be always waiting for something? listening as if for some summons?

Elizabeth remembered the story which she had gathered in the village the previous day concerning the battle which Henry of the Scar had seen fought in the heavens. And she told her husband. What should it mean? she questioned. Carl laughed strangely. 'O,' he said, 'Lord Otto is no better than a monk. He will never know from what quarter danger comes.'

It was just so that Rudolf, the strange Forester, had spoken—just so that he had laughed. Howbeit, for some brief space Carl worked again more in his fields and spent less of his time abroad. Life seemed to have gone back into its old channel, save for one thing which weighed heavy, though unacknowledged, on the housewife's heart. Not often now did she see her husband's former comrade, Willebald.

VI

Once more was Elizabeth sitting in her cottage, and it was very dark. She was alone: Carl had been gone since early morning. And it seemed to the peasant woman that once again some cloud descended from the sky, or some mist rose from the earth, to make the night ink-black and shut out all the stars. Presently an uneven step ascended their path, and a hand was laid upon the latch. A woman, by the step, and an old one, had entered the room, like one who could see in the darkness.

'Who is it?' said Elizabeth. 'Jutta, only old Jutta,' answered a voice, which she recognised. Whereupon she set herself to prepare the evening meal. All the while she was doing so Jutta was seated on the stool at the opposite corner of the hearthstone, between it and the wall: and she laughed low to herself:—'Ha-ha ha-ha-ha,' not loud, but evenly, and without ceasing. The fire fell upon her face, which was bent down. She rocked herself backwards and forwards. The lower part of her body was hidden by the raised hearthstone. 'Ha-ha-ha-ha-ha,' low, not loud. It was never any use to interrupt her: besides, it brought ill-luck to speak to her before she spoke. 'Ha-ha-ha-ha-ha'—till it began to get into a person's bones.

At last the old woman looked up into Elizabeth's face, and asked her old question: 'Where is Wicked Hilda, Elizabeth of the Corner? Have you found Wicked Hilda?'

'I know nothing of your Wicked Hilda,' said Elizabeth, though indeed she partly knew.

'That is not true,' answered the crone, and she laughed once more. 'That is not true—are you not Elizabeth the Out-born?' she added in a more questioning tone.

'What of her, then?' asked the other.

And at last, in broken fragments, but clearly enough to be understood, Elizabeth got from the woman the whole story, which it was reckoned unlucky even to hint at by most of the villagers of Lehndorf.

The new moon. Then it was known that the screech-owl came and sat upon one of the holy oaks which enclosed the village, and cried defiance to the priest of Lehndorf, the successor to him who had banned her for eternity. For the screech-owl was once a maiden of Rettenberg Castle, Hilda by name. In fulfilment of a vow, her father and mother had dedicated her to God. But she had a lover; and he collected a host to rescue her. Wherefore one night Rettenberg Castle was surrounded by a troop of horsemen all on black horses. Whence they came none knew. The castle was surprised; and Lord Herbert the Good and the Lady Wilhelmina were cast into a dungeon, and Hilda and her paramour ruled the land. But the peasants revolted, and sent over to the Emperor's court, at which lived another of the house of Rettenberg, the heir, should it prove that Lord Herbert was dead; and the new lord of Rettenberg came with troops furnished by Emperor Otto, and laid siege to the castle. Then it was that the priest of

Lehndorf had made procession thrice round the castle with uplifted cross and lighted tapers. And after the third round he read the ban* against the lovers, the book was closed, the bell was rung, and the tapers were blown out. That was the day of the New Moon. And that night the garrison broke through the camp of the besiegers and rode away, the lover with Hilda on his saddle-bow, and all his men behind him. All in black armour on black steeds. And many who saw them close declared that the nostrils of the horses glowed as if they were on fire within. Whither they went none had ever learned.

When Herbert and his wife were found, it was in a dungeon below the keep. They were bound with iron to two stakes. They had the hue of life but the coldness of death. And since then there had been a part of the forest, with all the Heath of the Three Pines beyond, which none entered willingly, and it was called Hilda's Land. Once a month, from the edge of that, or even on the gospel oak* within the village itself, Hilda, in the likeness of a screech-owl, screamed her defiance of the Priest of Lehndorf.

When Jutta had finished her story, she sat silent a while, as if listening. Then she spoke to herself, rocking backward and forward. 'The New Moon,' she said, 'the New Moon has just been born.' And Elizabeth knew for what she was listening, what she herself would hear, as she had heard it one month ago. At the thought thereof her blood turned cold.

'The New Moon,' said Jutta, 'the New Moon.' Then came, as Elizabeth knew that it would come, the long cry of the screech-owl. And in a little time the baying of a hound. Jutta raised her head a little. Her two eyes—almost all of her that was visible now in the dying firelight—seemed to grow larger and to glare like the eyes of a cat: and once again she laughed—not loud, but low, and even and long. 'It is not Carl that you are waiting for,' she said.

The words struck terror on Elizabeth, revealing depths in her soul which she had never sounded.

'It is not Carl for whom you fear, but Willebald.'

'It is false,' Elizabeth tried to say; but the words died unuttered.

'And they are coming, coming!' And even as Jutta said this, the baying of the hounds, the screaming of the owl, seemed to have left the shelter of the woods and to be coming towards them.

'I am lost, lost,' Elizabeth groaned to herself. She tried to feel terror for her husband's safety; for she knew, she knew not how, that he as well as Willebald were bound up with that sound of hounds and huntsmen which she heard driving through the darkness. All the time she felt within herself that it was for her husband's friend that her terrors went abroad. And now to her fancy Jutta's eyes grew greater and greater, and Jutta herself seemed to be towering—towering; while Elizabeth heard the low, even laughter repeated on all sides of her.

'They are coming, coming; but they will never come again!' So Jutta cried aloud. And then the shadowy form of a hound seemed to dress itself out of the darkness. Elizabeth instinctively stretched out her hand to touch it, remembering the touch of the hound once before the day that she fell against the hearth-stone. But this time darkness closed round her, and she lost consciousness.

VII

It was crazy Jutta who had told her daughter-in-law that Elizabeth of the Corner was ill of the fever: a proof, the village woman thought within herself, that Jutta was indeed a witch, for it was known that the beldame* had not left the house for a week. Another villager had gone and nursed Elizabeth. It was no wonder she should have fallen ill. For now it seemed that Carl of the Corner had disappeared. These things made Elizabeth a marked person; and when, after three days, she came once more to the fountain, the neighbours stood a little apart, and some whispered her history among themselves.

Carl's wife was debating whether she must not journey to the castle, or at least to one of the rangers' cottages, to find out if her husband had been taken for poaching. But then, to ask such a thing might betray him. As for the vision she had seen in her cottage, and the screeching of Hilda and the baying of hounds, she put these things as much from her thoughts as she could. Now, as she was still pondering in her mind, she saw old Walter, the head ranger, coming up to the village place itself, his boar spear in his hand, and his cross-bow on his back. Her heart sank. Now perhaps she should know, and know the worst that had happened to Carl and him.

No doubt many of the neighbours suspected the cause of Carl's and Willebald's disappearance, and divined Elizabeth's hopes and fears. When she and Walter met at the corner of the place, there came a pause in the talk round the fountain, and the water likewise paused in its splashing as if to listen. Even now she could not bring herself to begin the talk. But, when a greeting had passed, she stood before the ranger fingering her thread awkwardly, like a bashful girl. Her hand trembled, and the spindle struck her on the knees. The forester took pity on her.

'Is it sooth* I hear that Carl of the Corner is gone away?' he asked.

'I cannot say,' Elizabeth got out.

'Nay; but a villager may not be away more than two days, you know that, without the Bailey's* leave.'

'It is not his fault, nor—nor—Willebald's,' Elizabeth cried suddenly. 'If your Two Foresters had never come to our house it would all have been well. They it is who tempted them forth.' Now that her tongue was loosed, she stood before him wild-looking, flushed, and panting.

'How strangely she looks,' said some of the gossips. 'Send that she have not been bewitched!'

But Walter did not seem afraid. 'What foresters be they?' he asked.

'Gotschalk and Rudolf.'

'I have no rangers with such names. Stay, there is old Rudolf, the same that was disabled long since by a boar. But he no longer walks the woods. He hath a cottage of my lord, and——'

'Such they called themselves,' put in the other. 'And that they were foresters there was no mistaking—— Indeed,' she went on excitedly, 'I am sure they come for no good to my husband, but to tempt them away to hunt on the heath.'

'On the heath?' said Walter. 'But none save the Devil's rangers would hunt there.' 'I know not—— Perhaps they talked wildly—— I understood them to talk of the heath, and so did Carl—— He and Willebald would never go there.' But as she spoke she grew pale, and trembled, knowing how Willebald's rashness might tempt him to any enterprise.

'What manner of men were they?'

Elizabeth began in confused language to describe the two rangers, whom in truth she had never seen very distinctly by the firelight.

'Well, well,' said Walter, 'to-morrow is the rangers' day, when all meet in the morning at my house to take their commands for the week, and determine the ranges. It was in part for this matter that I came here to-day. For I could give commands that they would seek thy husband. But not unless you will. Come, then, to my house at sunrise, and you will see the twain you seek.'

But among the Freyherr's rangers were none like the two who had come to Carl's cottage on the eve of St. Justin, two and more months ago. And the next day the villagers said among themselves at the fountain:—'Elizabeth of the Corner is gone to seek her husband at the castle.'

'But she will not find him there,' said another. (Was it crazy Jutta who spoke?) 'Yet there she will find him.'

'What was it she spake of two foresters?' said a third. 'Two foresters that had long-bows at their backs, as they carried them in my grandsire's day——'

Of a sudden a thrill passed round the assembly. At last a

woman gave voice to the thoughts of the rest.

'What if they should be Hilda's Foresters?' she said.

'Crazy Jutta knows,' said a fifth, looking round to where the old crone sat. But crazy Jutta only nodded to herself, and laughed.

VIII

Elizabeth took the path that, almost from the cottage, began to clamber up alongside the wood; then left it again; and, descending a little, crossed a piece of common land. There at the moment Hansel and Bertha, the goose-boy and goose-girl, were tending their flocks hard by the edge of the forest. These were the last familiar faces that she saw. Even at the moment of her passing them, there came the first of three signs of ill-luck. A hare sprang almost from beneath her feet, and hopped away, as if it went on three legs only. She followed it, and plunged into the forest, which began with young trees of hazel and oak. And, ah! as she entered the shade, an owl flapped forth in broad daylight. This was the second sign; and anon, as she wandered farther, she found that the leaf trees were exchanged for a forest entirely of pines. And here all token of life seemed to have departed, until a raven, the bird of fearful knowledge, rose and circled thrice about her head, then, with a harsh cry, winged away. The three omens of mischance, the hare, the owl, and the raven! Her heart died within her.

And now the wood suddenly ceased, and she was at the foot of the castle hill. Like some vast winding stair, battlement succeeded battlement up the hillside. There were three gateways to pass, which might be likened to the landings on that winding stairway. Elizabeth remembered, as from afar off, some story she had heard of a man walking up such flights of stairs as these. Stairs were no part of her ordinary experience.

At the bottom of the first, it seemed to her she saw a huge Thing stretched out dragon-like and with mighty scales. In shape it was as a centipede. But it paid no heed to her, and she passed on.

At the second flight, a Figure all in steel was pushing against another Figure all in brown. 'The hunting-knife and the soup-ladle':—it was as if a voice within her said this. What a dust they raised! In spite of herself Elizabeth laughed. They, too, took no heed of her, and she passed on, and began to mount another stair.

At the third door was a Little Old Man. How long his nose! How keen his eyes! 'I know who you are,' thought Elizabeth. 'You are Godfather Death.' And, though she did not utter her thought, it seemed to her that the Old Man nodded, and smiled a lean smile, and let her pass on. She could have laughed again; for she knew now that she had strayed far away from the common earth.

When she had climbed the last flight, and reached the very courtyard of the castle keep, behold! all was changed once more, though it was not a whit more human or of this terrene life. The great dome of the sky spread over her, and seemed quite close, nothing else so near. Straight from above the walls of the court, which was dominated on one side by the keep, on another by the chapel, rose this mighty temple, the sky. Was it possible for men to abide so near the habitation of God, and live? If so, such men could not be of common mould. Elizabeth was afeared to think that she had ventured up to such regions. The three omens of the forest might be encountered. The three unearthly sights of the flights of stairs might be passed. This solemn and unchanging dome of heaven was more terrible than all.

As she stood, not so much thinking these things as by the sense of them bereft of thought, Freyherr Otto, of Retten-berg, came out of the castle. He was tall and not weakly built: rather, as it seemed, all strung of nerve and sinew, but with little flesh. His shoulders had a slight stoop, and his shaven face, save for the marks it bore of much exposure to the air, was almost the face of a priest. You would have said too that some flame of zeal had caught him: a dull fire burned in his eyes, his steel-shod feet grasped the stone of the steps as he descended. At the bottom it was as if of a sudden he grew conscious of the sky spread over him. He paused a moment with his eye raised as if in prayer. Two pages carried, one his helmet, the other his sword. A group of men-at-arms now showed in the doorway, and another figure, a veritable priest this time, appeared upon Elizabeth's right hand. He was younger than the Lord of Rettenberg, not more than thirty years of age, but thin, and pale, and with a worn face. He first took note of the woman standing in the court.

'What would you, my daughter?' he said.

Elizabeth could not find her voice. It was as if she had been translated from earth to heaven. 'I have, I would, father,' she was beginning; but now Lord Otto stepped forward to meet the chaplain. 'It has come, the time has come,' he cried, and the fire which had burned dull behind his eyes seemed to leap into sudden flame. 'The Holy War is proclaimed. To-day comes a message from our Lord the Emperor.'

'God's will be done,' was all the chaplain said. But he spoke rather to himself than to the Lord of Rettenberg, who went on unheeding:—'Come thou with me. To-night I depart with a hundred men to Treves. Arnulf, my ancient, comes after me with another hundred and provisions and arms——'

'But who will remain?'

'Rupert, the Seneschal, remains, and Walter, the Ranger. I have made him lieutenant in the castle.'

'It is not enough, my lord; remember——'

'None will attack us while the War of the Cross goes on.'

'No Christian men, perhaps——'

'You are thinking of the old wizard's prophecy? *You,* sir priest! Now come in, and prepare to administer to us ere we depart.'

The colloquy continued. But Elizabeth heard no more. The Freyherr and the chaplain both took their steps towards the chapel. Then the pages followed, and the men-at-arms, too, entered the building one by one. Presently she heard the voice of the priest intoning the service. She heard, too, a great braying of horns, a neighing of horses in the stable, shouts from lower down the hillside.

The court was once more nearly clear. But one or two soldiers still hung at the chapel door. Presently one of these sighted Elizabeth. 'But who is this woman?' he said. 'Ay, my faith, who is the woman?' said another. And they came down the steps towards her. She shrank a few paces back, and found herself against the wall.

'Whoever she is, she shall give a blessing to the crusade,' and the man caught hold of Elizabeth, and kissed her roughly. Now, for the first time since she entered the court did she remember fully her own identity, and what she had come there for. The first soldier had handed her on to his comrade, who held her in a still tighter embrace. She struggled in terror. At that moment the old man whom she had seen at the gate below passed by, and again he nodded and smiled his sour smile. 'Save me, save me, Godfather Death!' Elizabeth cried beside herself. And the two men let go of her, and began to laugh so loud that some other men-at-arms, who had been just inside the chapel porch, came out to see what was going on.

'Ha-ha-ha,' rang in Elizabeth's ears. It was the laughter of a demon. Her eyes could not move from a stone devil, who looked down at her from near the chapel roof. And then there was the great dome of the sky, lying close over all, weighing on all.

'But say who you are.' The man shook her roughly out of her half-trance.

'I am the wife of Carl—Carl of the Corner,' she answered panting, a sob at her throat.

'Carl of the Corner? who is he?'

'He is nothing,' said Godfather Death, speaking for the first time, and he nodded and smiled.

Elizabeth gave a scream. 'Hist,* a plague on you,' said

one of the men who had just come from inside the chapel. 'A plague on you,' said one of the first pair, and he struck her on the mouth. The castle walls closed round her, and the blue heavens seemed to descend upon her. Then she recovered herself to see only the Old Man still smiling and nodding.

'He is nothing here in this world,' he said; and then he pointed. And Elizabeth looked in the direction his finger took. And, behold! she could see over the battlements, and quite plainly as far as the Heath of the Three Pines. Nay, on looking again she saw two men hanging upon the centre one of the Three Pines, and two men standing under the tree. Then she strained her eyes a third time, and lo! she could see the faces of the two men standing: they were Gotschalk and Rudolf, the unknown Foresters. But, besides that, she could see the faces of the two dead men hanged by the neck upon the Pine itself, and they were the faces of Carl and Willebald. And yet the castle ramparts had been high above her head where she stood, and the Heath of the Three Pines lay far outside the skirts of the great forest, which surrounded the castle for miles.

IX

It was autumn now. The men and women of Lehndorf were taking their way by twos and threes, or in little companies, down alongside the river towards Andersbach Minster, for it was the eve of All Saints, the vigil of All Souls. There was to be a great office for the dead at the minster church that day: with doles,* as by custom, to some of the poor and aged of Lehndorf village—the two Lehndorfs, Lehndorf of Rettenberg and Abbot's Lehndorf—according to the bequest of Abbot John a century and a half ago. The Lord Archbishop of Treves, himself once Abbot of Andersbach, was to be at the office. He had just presented his old house with one of the new organs made by Master Cuno of Cologne, which spake, so men reported, now with the voice of all the angels, now with the roar of all the thunders of Sinai.

The villagers took their way by twos and threes, or in little companies, all save Elizabeth, Carl's widow, who went alone. For people were beginning to look at her a little askance. How had her husband died? None knew for certain; but there were many who could affirm. The story of the unknown foresters—Hilda's Rangers they were now freely called—had got about. Some in the village besides Elizabeth had heard the sounds of the mysterious Hunt, the scream of the screech-owl, the baying of hounds from the wood. The story went out that every new moon this Hunt swept by Elizabeth's door. Why, then, did she not come into the village? Was it indeed true that there was danger, was a sort of curse impending over that house of Carl's called the Corner? Others thought that the curse lay rather on Elizabeth's own blood. Was she not known to many as Elizabeth the Out-born? She did not get this name, certainly, because she herself had not been born in the village. But it was known, or said, by the older villagers that her father's mother had likewise been so called, and that about her origin there hung a mystery. Moreover, as all men knew, on great festivals of the church the Devil likewise is especially active: redoubled caution is necessary not to give him the shadow of an advantage, or instead of a blessing one might receive a greater damnation. It was on account of all these thoughts and rumours that Elizabeth was left to walk alone.

And she herself was tormented by thoughts which the villagers suspected not, or such suspicion would have increased their distrust. When she had almost persuaded herself that she was full of grief for the loss of her husband, Jutta's words would intervene in her memory:—'It is not Carl for whom you fear, but Willebald.' If to-night in her prayers, if to-morrow in the mass for the dead, she could not keep out Willebald from her heart, if in reality for him those prayers were said, the mass attended—was not this indeed to prepare the way to eternal fires? But then in the midst of those fearful thoughts would come a strange unreasoning hope, an obstinate conviction, do what she would to repress it, that Willebald was not dead: that he would emerge some day from the wood—some day when she was sitting alone at her cottage door. It was not true—what the villagers whispered—that every New Moon the Strange Hunt came out of the forest, and swept by that door. She had never heard the screech-owl's cry nor the hounds' baying since that dreadful evening when Jutta had been there, and had uttered the words:—'It is not Carl for whom you fear, but Willebald.' Words which Elizabeth could not help often repeating to herself. Dreadful words, fascinating as dreadful. Did some of the fascination extend to that evening's sounds? Did Elizabeth ever listen with a sort of hope mingled with her dread for the sound of the Strange Hunt coming from the wood, with a shadow of disappointment that it never came? Who shall say, when she herself could not have said?

X

Already the afternoon had turned to night. A lantern, whose flame was searched by the keen wind, hung by a rope before the minster's face. Another smaller light, a wick floating in oil, flickered not less before the face of the Virgin over the door within the huge porch. The wind was blowing gustily, and storms of autumn leaves whirled about the peasants' feet as they made their way into the minster. Once in, they stood huddled together at one end in almost complete darkness, waiting for the procession. At last the door to the abbey opened. Those who were nearest to the barrier on the north side could catch a glimpse of torches in the dim cloister. Then the procession came. First the lay-brothers and certain monks bearing candles and torches, and at once the farther end of the minster leapt into light. The tapers passed across the church, and partly disappeared behind the arch which separated that from the chancel. After the candle-bearers marched the rest of the monks, chanting as they marched. And last of all the auguster personages: the Lord Archbishop, in purple cassock and lace surplice, over whom four priests bore a baldaquin;* the venerable Abbot, whose robe was held by a monk; the Prior. These things Elizabeth beheld as in a dream. For a moment she was in fancy walking up the path by the side of the Lehen; and out of the wood at her right were sailing tiny candles, the tapers of the elves. That was at the beginning. The life that she had lived through since then—not yet six months ago—had held a world of fearful experiences, yet withal, withal....

The service had begun. Elizabeth's eyes were fascinated by the painted roof of the choir, for there the flickering smoking candles brought out a vision of angels' heads and wings which seemed to move, stars which seemed to shine and go out. Over her own head the roof had so far disappeared that she might have fancied herself in the open air. She was leaning against a heavy rounded pillar; and sometimes she forgot she was not leaning against some great oak of the forest. 'Or,' a voice seemed to say, 'against one of the Three Pines.' And at these words a mysterious wind blew through the wood in which she was: a wind that grew and grew into the sound of thunder, into a voice of doom. She shuddered, and shook herself awake.

A tuneful wind, a melodious thunder. It was the voice of the great organ blowing through the church. It rose louder and louder, sweeter and sweeter: there were voices, young ones, mingling with the sound. And now the choir breathed forth in a plaint of passionate sadness, as an autumn wind among pines; and now it answered in the thunder of a midsummer storm. 'Dare to disbelieve,' said the threatening voice of the organ. 'We do believe,' said the passionate wailing sound: 'Some sign, some sign!' Higher and higher the music seemed to rise and swell. It broke over Elizabeth like a mighty wave, until all her senses were submerged. She forgot her very existence. As the drowning mariner, when all his struggles are over, feels, with terror and unspeakable wonder, the waves breaking over him, which reverberate for ever on his dying senses: so she sank exhausted beneath that flood of sound. Her mind, which had battled all day with her feelings, trying to understand them, trying to control them, ceased to fight. The harmonies whelmed her, and she dropped upon her knees.

Then, as the mariner wakes from his death-sleep, to find that he has descended into a new world—the unsearchable depths of ocean: where gentle, wide-eyed creatures move amid forests, which are not of earth, and all the air (*Is* it air?) is of a weird dimness, and beats for ever with strange reverberations: so did Elizabeth now awake, no longer upon earth, nor lifted up into heaven, but wandering in a region which she had never entered before. Now she understood that solitary journey of hers to the castle; the goose-boy and goose-girl whom she had met at the entry of the forest. She understood the strange sights she had seen on the castle stairs, knew who was Godfather Death. All that journey no more seemed fraught with horrors as it had done only—when? She could not remember. Those elves, too, carrying tapers—they had been leading her on to this! All that had come and gone had been of their doing, and this, too, she understood now—she could not have said how or why.

Still the music breathed. But now suddenly, across all this splendour of melody, came a commonplace sound. A noise of knocking, as of a hammer. Clang, clang, ting, ting, went the monotonous mechanic noise. Elizabeth, awake once more to the world about her, looked round to see if any one else showed signs of hearing it. No one did. Yet still it continued, clang, clang, ting, ting, sharp, not loud, regular, mechanic. For all that, was it indeed a sound of earth? What a change that knocking wrought in her? From the place where she stood she commanded a good view of the Lord Archbishop of Treves, partly framed by the round arch which led from the church into the choir. He sat there, raised above the heads of the singing monks. Yet how small he was, this potentate of the church! A clamant fancy seized Elizabeth that he was but a figure carved in wood.

XI

And ever since that night at Andersbach Minster, Elizabeth was changed. She went seldom into the village now except of necessity. She chose for her washing, or for drawing water at the fountain, the hours when the other gossips were at their dinner. When, each week, she took her spool of thread to barter to John Franzel, the Weaver of Andersbach, she went up by a path which skirted above the other houses, and then descended towards where Franzel stationed his cart on the farther side of the village. For all that, though she would often sit at the door of her cottage looking toward the forest and, to see her, one would have said that she was listening for something, and waiting, her heart was full of terror. She dreaded, yet expected, some day to see the Two Foresters come forth. She had dreams of seeing the boughs part, and her husband and Willebald emerge with, not the hue of life but rather, the blueness of death on their faces, and with ropes round their necks. Thus she had seen them in that fearful vision from the castle ramparts.

She was sitting one afternoon, when she could no longer see the woods, so close enfolded was she in a November mist—light and grey, cold, deadening all sound. Now and then a broken branch crashed down unseen, echoing dully. Then silence came back heavy as before. Of a sudden—Christ in Heaven!—what noise was that? Something, Elizabeth knew, for which she had been waiting. Yet after all only a common forest sound. So at least she said to herself. But was it? It was in truth nothing but a knocking, knocking. Clang, clang, ting, ting, regular, mechanic.

Never now did Elizabeth sleep in the bed which she had been used to share with her husband. The gallery in which it stood was unvisited, and lay thick with dust. Always now she slept on the settle. This night she slept and dreamed. It seemed to her that she was standing beside a little stream in the forest. And facing her, upon the other side of the stream, was a high rock. She had never seen the place; that she recognised even in her dream: recognised it with one hand as it were, and with the other seemed to claim familiarity with the spot. There, at any rate, she knew that she had to stand and wait, even if she waited for eternity. And, as the word flashed into her thoughts, she seemed as if she could never remember the time that she had not waited there. Then she started in her sleep; for there came from inside the rocky wall a regular sound—clang, clang, ting, ting, a knocking, knocking. It seemed that a pigeon flew down from a tree bearing a golden key in its beak. Then for a moment the dream became confused. The next thing she saw was a little snake gliding along the grass towards the stream? or along the floor of her room?—which? She started broad awake, and found the light of morning stealing through the hole under the roof.

The dreary day and its hard toil had returned. But—surely she had not over night left the chamber swept and clean, as she saw it now? Not a crust nor a bone was on the floor. And the wood, too, piled ready for the hearth. Had she cut it? She could not remember. But, if not she, who had done this thing? Was it possible that Carl had come back again? She said 'Carl' to herself; but her inmost thoughts were not of her husband. Had she not always been waiting for that one to return?

Another time, Elizabeth seemed in her dreams to hear the lowing of Tecla, and to say to herself:—'That is a good omen: all will be well.' When she woke in the morning—behold! the milk had been drawn in the pail; and that for certain she could not have done the night before. She trembled; but in part with expectation and hope.

Ever after that life became more and more easy to her. Unseen hands shook down the dried ferns, the litter for the cattle; they drew the milk. In the cold winter mornings the unseen house-spirit walked up to the cascade in the brook, the one place which was never frozen, but where the villagers never used to go, and filled her pail there. The neighbours, who beheld her from their fields, wondered to see a woman sitting idle at the cottage door so often when the sun shone. Sometimes she let her spinning wheel rest. Yet had she longer strands of yarn to barter with Franzel Weaver than any other woman in Lehndorf. Sometimes he paid her in silver. And this she carefully hoarded in a secret hole beneath the settle.

Ever in her dreams and in her thoughts she saw the little serpent coming to her cottage from the way of the wood. And something within her told her that the serpent was Willebald; till one night, when she had laid down to dream, she saw in her dream, as heretofore, the house-door, which she locked at night, open of itself and the little snake come gliding through. This time he had something shining in his mouth. And, on the morrow morning, with a pang of immense desire and immense terror, behold! among the straw of her bed the woman found something glittering, and it was a piece of gold—such as she had never seen before. An inner voice spoke to her, and seemed to tell Elizabeth that this was the fatal moment of her life: that she might yet be saved, if she would not take this money, but would throw it away. And in obedience thereto, she ran out in the cold frosty morning meaning, thinking she meant, to fling the ducat into the brook. She held the coin tight in her fist, and kept her fist behind her. But, behold, her foot slipped; in seeking to save herself she dropped the coin; and it rolled away into a crevice beneath a stone, and lay there, only one pin-point of its rim catching the light.

There, then, let it lie! Elizabeth went back to her cottage with a heavy heart. She had, she hoped, she feared, taken the decisive step. No more would unseen hands do half her household drudgery, nor would they spin at night while she lay cosily abed. That little heap of silver in the hole would never grow larger now. Never again in her life should she possess a coin of gold. What, perhaps (she could not tell), was worse than all, never again would she dream of the friendly coming of that little snake whom in her thoughts she had christened

Willebald. She tried to think that morning that she could not, if she wished, find the precise spot where she had fallen down, or the exact stone under which the ducat had rolled. She tried to pray and to occupy herself with pious thoughts. But in the midst of these efforts she remembered that some snow had been on the ground when she walked towards the brook, so that her footsteps would be preserved. At that she started from her seat by the hearth and opened the door. Ah! It was snowing again now: soon those footsteps would be obliterated. It was Our Lady herself who had sent the snow—the feathers from her bed.

'Not so,' said a voice, 'but Frau Hilda!' She started, and looked round the room. There was no one in it. But she did not always know whether the voices she heard were from inside her or from outside. 'Quick, quick,' said the voice again. 'She sent the snow for you in the night: but she sends it against you this morning. You may lose your luck for ever.' And, indeed, the footsteps leading from the door were already half effaced.

Elizabeth hesitated no more. She went back along the steps she had made that morning, and behold! not yet hidden by the snow, for it lay under the ridge of the stone, the edge of gold shone out like a star in the whiteness. All her struggles were over: the Peace of the Wicked fell upon her soul. She cherished the gold coin as if it had been a child, and placed it among her little hoard of silver. How radiantly it showed, like a queen among her subjects! Twenty times that day did Elizabeth stoop down under the settle, and lift the stone in the wall which concealed her treasury.

A week after she dreamed the same dream again, and in the morning another golden ducat was hidden in the straw. Then it was twice a week, and before the summer was come, no morning passed but she found one. And full of a wonderful new experience, the possession of a treasure, did she go about in those days, as the year dropped to its close.

XII

In Lehndorf village folk had begun to say that Elizabeth had the Evil Eye. Once she had a quarrel with Peter Pinner's wife; and the next day the woman fell sick and soon died. Black Riechen's boy had, as ill-taught boys will, thrown a stone at Elizabeth from behind a hedge. She seemed not to so much as turn and discover who was the delinquent. For all that, ere the New Moon came round, the child fell into his mother's well, and was drowned. Wherefore, all men greeted kindly Carl's widow of the Corner. But few of them, and that seldom, came up the path to her door. And when she went forth to wash or to draw water, the people in the Place would slink away one by one. But she recked* little of these things. She held her head high among her neighbours. One thing was ever in her thoughts, the growing pile of golden ducats, which made a treasure great enough to buy up all the houses in Lehndorf.

The boys followed her at a distance, and peered at her round the corners of houses, from the edges of the wood, snatching a fearful joy. 'There she goes,' they said one to another, 'Elizabeth the Out-born.' Now this name was almost always bestowed on her. Her nearest neighbours, Peter Ploughman and his wife, saw her go past their door, which was ajar, the firelight shining out upon the snow: she, a black figure mounting up in the night greyness towards her cottage, which stood apart from the others, and dominated most of them. 'But how,' said Peter's wife, 'doth not the Devil come, and carry her away, when she still dares to come to Mass?' 'Nay, nay,' said Peter, more charitably. For he had been friends with Carl and his wife in days gone by.

Elizabeth on her side went untroubled by thoughts of the gossips. She had little work to do now. There stood the wood stacked for the firing, there was the iron pot ready for use, the grain was there, and the milk to mix therewith. Tecla gave

twice as much as heretofore. If in those days it had been possible to turn milk into money, Elizabeth would have spared to
use but a little of it for her porridge. But such a thing was not
possible, so she ate royally of milk and porridge and cheese.
Though there was little to do, she grew impatient of what had
to be done, and could scarce bring herself to light the fire and
warm up the supper. For all that it must be said that she put
thus much restraint upon herself that she would not touch
it till the supper was done. Then, but not till then, she drew
it from its retreat. To lengthen out the joy of her task, she
always first enforced herself to count the silver pieces, though
for many days their number had remained the same. There
were thirty-nine. How deliciously each piece rang ting, ting,
as she tinkled it on the hearth-stone! Instinctively she parted
the hoard into little heaps, thirteen in each. Then at last she
set to work upon the gold, and the ducats glanced like a company of princes in the glow of the fire, and rang like the mailed
feet of knights upon the hearth. And of these there were one
hundred and sixty-nine, and they made thirteen companies of
thirteen. Clang, clang, they had sounded as she dropped them
on the slab. And now it seemed to Elizabeth that she heard an
answering clang, clang, from underground. Her heart glowed
with delight. It meant that they were forging her fresh pieces!

One, two, three, four, five, six, seven. . . . She counted them
all over again. Thirteen whole companies; thirteen in each.
The room was as full of shadows as of light, as it must be when
the sole illumination comes from a wood fire. Looking up,
she was scarce surprised to see a shadow moving (it seemed)
slowly along the wall. Yes; the light was fitful, yet not so fitful
but that she could be sure the shadow had moved out of its
place in the corner, and noiselessly slid along the wall toward
the stool on which she sat.

Now, for a moment the firelight leapt up into bright flame.
During one instant Elizabeth still beheld the shadow, not
moving now, but more distinct than ever. It had the shape of
a woman with long hair, and as it were a helm upon her head.

Then the flame fell for ever; the fire had died out. All the shadows in the room assembled together to make a complete darkness.

XIII

The night after, no serpent came to her in her dreams. Nor did she find any gold piece in her bed. In the morning she turned over every straw and looked in every corner. Then she took out her hoard, and counted it twice over. For, she thought, maybe the serpent had found his way directly thereto from under ground. She listened for the clang of the elfin hammers, but in lieu thereof her ear was vexed by the sound of a bell. Now, as long as a bell tolls, the Spirits of Earth and Air are powerless. Nor did Elizabeth once remember that this one was tolling the Christ made flesh upon the altar, and that she had stayed in her cottage, nor ever gone to Mass, that Sunday morning.

'What will Gebhard, the Priest, do now?' said the folk of Lehndorf. For now there were few in Lehndorf but deemed it certain that there dwelt among them one who was in league with the Evil Spirit.

In sleep the ensuing night, Elizabeth the Out-born once more saw her serpent. Yet was he changed. He bore no piece of money in his mouth; but, as it seemed, a bright spark flamed in his forehead. And now for the first time—but still sleeping—she spoke to the serpent. 'O, Willebald!' she called out. 'Is that indeed you?' 'It is I,' answered the snake. And she knew the voice. 'Come,' next spake the serpent, 'and follow me.'

Whether it were in the flesh or no, Elizabeth rose from her settle and passed in his wake out under the stars. How brightly they gleamed! Not in one colour neither, but white and green and blue, red and yellow. It must have been very cold. But Elizabeth did not feel it. Now they had entered a portion of the forest unknown to her. The little snake went quickly on before. At length they came to a brook: perhaps the same brook which flowed not far from Elizabeth's cottage, and from which the villagers had a tradition that it was unlucky to draw water. She looked upon the grass; and there, mildewed and rusted, lay Carl's old boar-spear, the one which he had left behind when he suddenly ran away after hearing Willebald's dream; and by its means the serpent, who had declared that he was indeed Willebald, crossed the stream, and Elizabeth walked through the water after him. And she knew the place for the same that she had seen in her dream. The bare rock rose before her, and barred her path. Now her companion, the serpent, disappeared in a crevice of the rock, and she stood there alone. Thereupon, behold! a pigeon flew down to her, as she had seen it in her dream—bearing a golden key in its beak. And, 'Fit this key into the wall of rock,' said the bird. 'There,' and it showed a hole, 'and it will open.'

The next moment she was in a vast cave. The roof thereof was arched like the roof of a church immeasurably great, and pillars on every side held up the roof. 'This,' said Elizabeth to herself, 'is the place which Willebald saw. It is——' 'The Devil's Minster.' The words came to her as if spoken from without. 'Then why,' she thought, 'am I not more afraid?' Perhaps because she saw a well-known, long unseen shape drawing near. On all sides among the pillars beneath the innumerable arches were moving lights. Only in the approaching figure did she see of what nature the lights were. More and more clearly, as he drew near, and with a heart beating more and more, she recognised Willebald. His face shone, strangely illuminated by a point of light, which nestled in his thick hair.

'Surely,' Elizabeth thought, 'that must be a jewel.' She remembered the description which he had given Carl of the gems, which shone like sparks of flame; and it seemed to her as if once more she gazed on the stars in the night sky, burning white and green, blue, red, and yellow.

Willebald took her hand. In and out among the pillars, beneath the arches, he led her to a hall which was like the chancel of the Minster Church at Andersbach, only far greater. Here, moreover, she saw no angels' heads or wings in the roof. On a throne in this great chancel, much as she had seen in the other church the Archbishop of Treves, sat an Old Man with a wise and terrible face. 'Welcome,' he said to Elizabeth, and he nodded his head. 'We have waited for you a hundred years.' And a murmur of assent went round the choir. 'Why have you brought me here?' Elizabeth said to Willebald. Her companion did not answer. But the Old Man spoke again. 'It was fated so,' he said. 'Do not you know who you are? from whom descended? Listen.'

'Listen,' said the Old Man of the wise and terrible face. 'Once there was a young knight who rode through Rettenberg Forest. He came none knew whence nor whither he was going. And in the deepest part of the wood he met a maiden. She knew not how she had wandered into the wood. But while she was there, and thought she must starve to death, there had flown down to her a pigeon which bore a silver key in its bill. The bird said to her:—"With this key open yonder tree, and thou wilt find all the food thou needest." She opened the tree, and found milk and bread. Presently came another pigeon, with another key, and it said:—"Dost thou see yonder tree? Open it, and thou shalt find a bed." And this, too, she found. And the next morning came a third pigeon with a silver key, and it said:—"Dost thou see yonder tree? Open it, and thou shalt find rich clothes." And this happened as with the other trees. This alone the maiden knew; nor could she remember how long she abode in the forest. Then the knight stayed with her in the wood. At last a child was born to her. But the knight went away. And the mother at last found her way to the village of Lehndorf. There she died. But the child of her lived. And because none knew its parentage or coming it was called Elizabeth the Out-born; and of this Elizabeth you are descended.'

'But who was the maiden?' asked Elizabeth.

'She was the heiress of Rettenberg,' answered the Old Man. 'And for this cause must you join our company. For now the time is almost come for the attack on Rettenberg Castle. Hilda shall lead it, and the Army of Blankenroth moves up to the attack according to the old prophecy. But the attack could never be made until an offspring of Hilda of Rettenberg was found in the flesh willing in the flesh to join the band. You are she. . . .'

'A child of the Wicked Hilda?'

'Of her whom the peasants of Lehndorf call the Wicked Hilda. You were once of them and spoke their language. You are so no more. Behold I give you the token of those who are chosen.' And he placed a jewel on her head.

Even as he spoke Elizabeth knew that she was changed, that she was no longer and never would be again the peasant woman tending her kine, turning her thread upon the spindle, cooking the supper for her husband. Carl was far from her thoughts; even Willebald was half-forgot. She lifted her head proudly, and the jewel which she wore flashed like a flame.

In the morning there lay in her bed a bright point like that she had seen in her vision. This, she thought, is the jewel: and she took it in her hand. Of a truth there must have been some mystic virtue in the gem; for the longer that Elizabeth handled it the less like a peasant woman did she feel. Moment by moment she seemed to herself to grow in pride and in strength. And she ceased to count her other treasures from this day.

XIV

Children had died in the houses, cattle in the stalls. Hay had rotted in the stacks, corn had mildewed in the fields. It was an evil year with Lehndorf. No one now rejoiced that the Frey-herr was far away.

Two years and more had passed since Lord Otto left the castle, and set out to join the army of the Crusade. No news had come to Rettenberg or to Lehndorf of him or of the army which the Emperor led to Palestine. Now the evil year was setting to its close. ' "Tis the winter of Blankenroth,' Jutta had been heard to say. The words had an ill-omened sound, whatever precisely she might have meant by them. The holy time of the Nativity came round, the dreadful time of the Twelve Days, when the Unseen of Earth and Air have redoubled powers. As all men now believed, they had a fearful ally among visible mortals; and this Christmas morning, as in the darkness the early bell began to toll for the Mass, men were debating, in themselves or with others, whether Elizabeth of the Corner would indeed brave Heaven by coming to the Mass of the Nativity; or would dare to absent herself on this day of days, as she had done for a month or more.

'They say,' Peter Ploughman's wife had said the evening before, 'that to-morrow she will not come to Mass. We shall see.' Like many another she listened more keenly than her wont for the first voice of the morning bell, and got ready quickly to take her way to the little church. And now ensued the first of many strange tokens, that happened that day. For when the bell had sounded only a few times, of a sudden it stopped ringing. Some men ran to the church to know the cause. There stood Wishart the Sacristan, his eyes wide open, grasping the rope, but making no effort to pull the bell. The villagers shook him; and though his eyes were wide open, he had been fast asleep. Perhaps it was nothing but the great cold. . . .

Now the villagers were standing huddled together in the little dark church. It was lighted by two small windows only, narrow and round-topped. There was no window in the chancel, which was lower than the rest of the chapel and round-arched like the windows. The east end, the walls, the ceiling of the chancel were painted with a representation of the Day of Doom. There stood the folk, huddled in the morning twilight. Old Gebhart by the illumination of one smoking torch began the Mass. The people peered about them, and saw no Elizabeth. 'Kyrie Eleison,' intoned the priest. 'Kyrie Eleison,' sang the Sacristan and the two Choristers. Wishart had put a live coal into the censer, and Poldsel began to incense the priest. He swung the censer to and fro, but neither smoke nor smell came out: then he glanced inside, and behold! the coal had gone dead black. 'Twas too late to rekindle it; and no one of the villagers could see what was being done.

Now Gebhart, the good old man, took out the pyx.* More zealously the boy swung his censer. John, the acolyte, had gone to the bell. Alas! what had happened? The priest let fall the monstrance. At the same moment a light laugh passed round the church over the heads of the worshippers. The priest picked up the fallen monstrance, and on went the service. 'Sanctus, sanctus, sanctus, Dominus Deus Sabaoth,' he chanted. The choristers and villagers chanted back; while John the Acolyte pulled the bell, and the sick and bedridden of Lehndorf waited to hear its holy sound. But instead of the tolling which drives away all evil spirits, what sound was heard? The noise of a knocking, as of a hammer on an anvil, not loud, but regular, mechanic! O, what could these things portend?

Who was to bring to account the cause of such strange doings—the instrument, rather? Who was to make accusation? 'If Lord Otto were but here!' some said. But Lord Otto was far away.

XV

Hans, Simon Forester's son, did a bold thing. For on the Night of the Three Kings he crept up alone to Elizabeth's cottage determined to spy upon her doings. Much had her case been talked over in the village. Hans had been challenged to do the thing he set about.

He walked up the path by the edge of the wood; and as he went, his feet crunched in the snow. Every shadow which lay across the whiteness seemed a live thing, and the blackness thereof was shot with a shifting red as of flames. Yet still he kept on; he gained the very door; with trembling hand he lifted the latch. Next moment he stood transfixed with dread of what might be to come. Howbeit he saw at the first nothing stranger than the mistress of the cottage bending over her hearth. She was passing something—bright sparks—from hand to hand. A witch at least!

For all that Hans said to himself such a sight had no great terrors. But, even as he tried to reassure himself, he was aware of something else. He had noted, as he supposed, Elizabeth's shadow black against the cottage wall. Now the Shadow began to move. It glided along the wall, drawing ever nearer and nearer to the bending figure. And while his eyes were fascinated by this sight, and he was turned so cold that he could neither move nor cry, behold! from another corner another Shadow stole in like fashion along another wall. Another followed it; and then another. Then of a sudden Elizabeth of the Corner raised herself. But was it indeed Elizabeth? Hans felt that she looked like some dreadful queen. She held up the jewels, which were now grown into one tiara of gems, and placed the glittering band on her forehead. Then she spoke. 'Come out if you will,' she said. Hans trembled and almost sank to the earth. But it was not to him the words were spoken. For one by one the Shadows came out from the walls. In shape like women, young, not old. Did they not wear helmets on their heads, and their dusky hair sweep down from beneath the casques? And Hans unseen heard the voices of the mortal woman and of those dusky Shapes asking and answering.

'I have seen you before,' said Elizabeth.

'We have been always with you,' said the First Shadow.

'Who are you?' asked the woman.

'We are the Daughters of Earth and Gloom,' answered the Shapes.

'What would you with me?'

'You are of us. We have been always near you, for from our land do you come, and are of our territory. We brought you back thereto. From the day you married Carl, and came to live in this house, we have watched over you. We brought you here, we brought Willebald to you . . .' Here Elizabeth shuddered. 'We sent the Two Foresters to take them both away again. For now you have nought more to do with Carl or with Willebald. The time has come to join our company.'

'O, I am afear'd,' cried Elizabeth. One of the Shadows stretched forth her hand and took Elizabeth's. 'You *were* afear'd,' it said. And Hans, the Forester's son, beheld the face of her who had been a peasant woman. It was more than ever like the face of some dreadful queen.

'You ride with us to-night,' said the Shadow which had last spoken. ''Tis the night for which we have waited a hundred years.'

'Am I then to fight under Hilda's banner?' asked Elizabeth; for still she shuddered at that name.

'You fight *with* Hilda, under the banner of a greater than she. Of One whom we do not name.'

And as he heard those words Hans, the Forester's son, trembled so violently that he was like to fall. 'See now,' said another of the Dark Maidens, 'the signs in the Northern Sky.' Hans turned himself round at the words. Behold! all the sky before his face was suffused with red, and one moment it seemed to him that out of the glow there upreared itself a spectral Shape, in plume and harness red, on a red steed. But along all the horizon—all that he could see—coursed black clouds trailing towards the earth. In two great semi-circles they seemed moving towards him. It was but during one second that he beheld this vision. 'Who is that who has dared to place himself at the door?' said a hollow voice behind him. He did not pause, nor turn to see the speaker: he rushed forward from where he stood, sliding and stumbling breathlessly in the darkness down the path he had mounted. He dared not so much as raise his eyes. Yet he seemed to be aware that the coursing clouds now swept close by him; and once from out of them came a strange sound—a horse's neighing.

No one in the village was in wait to hear Hansel's report. Yet, though it was now deep in the night, not a soul was abed or in his house. They all stood huddled in the Place by the talking fountain, whispering fearfully and pointing trembling fingers towards the northeast—towards Blankenroth. ' 'Tis indeed thither it lies,' said one, shivering as he spoke. 'It is the army that is marching from Blankenroth.' 'But—but not an army of men,' shivered another. 'Would it were!'

The wind had begun to howl. The red light darted up into the sky. Some heard a whinnying sound come through the air or along the ground. Yet there was nothing visible. Then for the first time a woman screamed with terror. Another and another followed her; till it was enough to make a bold man's blood run cold. 'O mercy!' 'O Mary Mother!' 'O Jesu, save and protect us!' 'Where is Gebhard, the priest!' 'Where is Walter, the forester!' they cried. Then came one running, white with terror, to say that Gebhard, the good old man, had been found strangled in his bed.

XVI

'One who has been for the last time bold,' answered another of the Dark Maidens. 'And now, behold! the steeds are at the door.' Then, giving her hand to Elizabeth, she led her from the cottage.

Those that were black clouds in the sky, as they swept to earth before her door took, Elizabeth saw, shapes as nine rider-less steeds. She and her eight companion Shadows mounted upon them, and one set a helmet on her head. And no sooner was this done than behold! all the horizon of Heaven seemed filled with like companies—dark maidens on dark horses. Before them went the screech-owl's cry, no longer harsh to her ears but musical, like the music of a chant. And now the chant was sounding on all sides of her, they were singing the Night-riders' song:—

> Nine nines of maidens
> Ride to the maiden's moot
> On the burnt hill;

And ONE before them goes.
Black the steeds that bear them.
Their horses shake themselves,
And from their manes there fall
Dews in the deep dales,
Upon the high hills hail,
But in the underworld sparks of flame.

This is the Night-riders' song, and Elizabeth sang it as she was
borne away from Lehndorf.

XVII

Too late came the Abbot of Andersbach, with cross and
candles, and all his choir chanting after him as he marched. For
when the villagers had joined the march—for, though 'twas a
terrible thing to enter Rettenberg Forest, it was more dreadful to separate oneself from the holy band—they proceeded
through the deep wood toward the castle. Of a sudden the
forest cleared, and in a much wider circle of open country
than of old, behold! the hill which should have been the castle-
hill came into view. Only now no castle was there. A bare hill,
no more: save that on the summit grew Three Pines.

III

THE FOUR STUDENTS

A BARE attic room; on a wooden table one candle only in a wooden candlestick, and the candle was in snuff. Raynaud paused in his reading for the bad light, and Gavaudun snuffed the wick with his fingers. Then they all remained for a moment pensive, listening to the sounds of the night. For the wind had arisen again, and the leaded windows rattled; and from below came the monotonous low groan of the street lamp swaying to and fro upon its chain. The room, which the four students shared in common, contained little else save their four truckle beds,* beside each of which stood a pail for washing purposes. There were four chairs and the wooden table, round three sides of which they were sitting, close against the fire, for the night was bitterly cold. Blank darkness looked in upon them through the two lattice windows, which had neither shutter nor blind. The house had once been a hotel standing in its own grounds, but was now compressed into the Rue Pot-de-Fer, close to the corner where that street ran into the Rue des Postes. It lay in the quarter much frequented by Parisian students, just outside that densely packed district known in those days as l'Université. At the end of their street, beyond its junction with the Rue des Postes and at the end of the Rue des Postes itself, stood two of the thousand barriers which shut in Paris proper.

It was in the winter of 1787. The world without, though these four recked little of it, was in a ferment, nominally because the King's Minister, Loménie de Brienne, was at loggerheads with the Parliament of Paris; really because the times were big with much greater issues which no man then foresaw.

The wind softened a little, the windows rattled less, and Raynaud took up his book again. It was a book which he had bought that day off a stall on the Petit Pont. Le Bossu du Petit Pont, as the keeper of the stall was called, was a familiar figure to most of the students of that quarter. On examination it proved to be the work *De Invocatione Spirituum*, by Johannes Moguntiensis, or John of Menz; a man whom Cornelius Agrippa speaks of several times in his *Philosophia Occulta*, and in his familiar letters, as having been in some sort his master. Raynaud read on, and the others,—Sommarel, Gavaudun, Tourret—listened rather languidly to the Latin of the magician, as he set forth the processes by which might be formed between two, three, or four persons (but best of all if they were four) a mystic chain so called, 'each one with the others,' and how the supernal powers were to be conjured to aid the work. The author was at once prolix and obscure; and none of the four, not even the reader, paid strict attention to his words.

'But, hold!' said Tourret; 'what did you say? *In Vigilâ Nativitatis*—why it is precisely the Eve of Noel that we are in to-night.'

'And so it is! If we were to try the charm?' said Gavaudun.

'Excellent! we will do so.'

'John of Menz come to our aid!' said Sommarel, folding his hands.

'Tush! You don't invoke John of Menz,' said Gavaudun. 'Let me see, whom have we got to call upon?'

'Oh, *Diabolus,* I suppose, or the *Anima Mundi*, the Soul of the World,' said Tourret.

'Nonsense,' said Gavaudun, who had taken up the book.

Glad of a little change they all rose up. 'We have to inscribe a pentacle, the Pentacle of Mars, on the floor,' said Raynaud. 'Then prick our arms and transfer the blood from one vein to another, he directs.'

'No, you say the incantation or conjuration first,' said Gavaudun, as he turned back to an earlier page. As he did so a sort of tune seemed to be running in his head. They scratched the pentacle on the floor with a rusty iron nail, and each took his stand in one of the angles. Then Gavaudun shouted out the conjuration:—'I conjure and require you,—Ja, Pa, Asmodai, Aleph, Beleph, Adonai, Gormo, Mormo, Sadaï, Galzaol, Asrael, Tangon, Mangon, Porphrael!'* It was not precisely thus that the words were written; but they seemed to come out of his mouth in this sort of chant; and all the four took it up and sang, 'Galzael, Asrael, Tangon, Mangon, Porphrael!' till the roof echoed. Then they stopped suddenly and stared at one another. They were all in a sweat; but each one laughed. Of course that was part of the joke; the other three had been roaring like that for a joke, but each one felt that for himself the chanting had been a mere contagion, had come out of him without his will.

'*O vos omnes spiritus terreni, invocamus et convocamus vos!* Ye spirits of the earth, we call and conjure you! Be ye our aiders and confederates, and fulfil whatever we demand!' Gavaudun with a solemn mien pronounced this prayer. 'Now for the drop of blood!' And he turned round to the table to re-read the passage of John of Menz. He seemed to take the lead now, while Raynaud did everything in a reluctant, half-mechanical way as one walking in his sleep. They had all been sitting without their coats, as the custom was in those days; two in loose dressing-gowns, one in a light jacket, and one in shirt sleeves. As they stood in the pentacle they took off these outer garments, or turned up the sleeves of them to bare their arms. Each one made with his penknife or stiletto a small incision in his arm, a little blood was squeezed out, according to the prescription, and exchanged against a drop of blood from his neighbour's arm, which, as well as it might be, was conducted into the wound made to receive it. It took time; for each one had to make the exchange with his neighbour; each had to make two pricks upon his arm, for only so could he be sure that he had not squeezed out again the foreign blood just imported.

'Quick!' said Sommarel. 'It is near twelve, and the whole must be done on the Eve of the Nativity.'

'There ought to be five of us,' said Tourret, 'to fill all the five angles.'

'No; it specially says not more than four. I suppose the Terrestrial Spirit, whose names we have been reciting, fills up the fifth angle.'

'Why Raynaud and I have not exchanged yet,' said Gavaudun, as the others held out their hands to complete the mystic circle.

'*Bon Dieu*, we cannot wait any longer. You see it is just twelve.'

They linked hands and shouted once more in chorus, and to the self-same chant: 'Ja, Pa, Asmodai, Aleph, Beleph, Adonai, Gormo, Mormo, Sadaï,' and the rest. Louder and louder they called, the sweat pouring down their foreheads. A wanderer of the night, supperless in the bitter cold, looked up at their windows which shone like a high beacon, heard the shout, and in his heart cursed those jovial revellers as he supposed them to be. Then from the neighbouring church of St. Genevieve rang over the compact mass of roofs the first notes of the clock, and next a chime of bells. Raynaud tore his hands from the others; a look of terror was in his face.

'That was famous!' said Sommarel, bursting into a laugh.

II

This room in the Rue Pot-de-Fer was for the four students no more than an inn on the high road of life. In six months they had separated again, and gone their different ways. It was now nearly six years since they had lived together in that room. Gavaudun had left Paris to become a professor at Lille, and, young as he still was, was a man already distinguished. On the capture of Lille he had become an Austrian subject, and had left Revolutionary France forever. Sommarel was practising the law in his native town. Tourret had married a rich wife and had disappeared from ken. Only Raynaud remained behind in the old room.

Since the four had parted the Revolution had begun, and had marched along its appointed way. At first Raynaud had taken his share in all the excitement of the time. He had been among the crowd when the Bastille fell. He had followed the procession of women to Versailles, and seen the King carried to Paris in triumph. But during the last two years all energy seemed to have ebbed from him; and a fantastic pageant of events had passed him, he himself taking no part in what was going forward, scarcely even heeding it. Time after time the faubourg of St. Marcel hard by had risen in black wrath, had flowed out in its thousands to meet St. Antoine, to meet the Marseillais volunteers, to whirl and eddy round the Tuileries and the Hall of the National Convention; or had gone forth in frantic joy to take part in I know not what Feast of the Revolution, Feast of Reason, Fraternal Supper, as the occasion might be; and had flowed back again, neither the better nor the worse in its every day life for all its wild exhibitions of rage and hope. Over all this Raynaud looked from his high citadel as if he had no concern in these terrene matters. But his indifference was not born of philosophy, only of a strange dulness which he could not shake off.

He had remained the constant inhabitant of the same room. But not always its sole occupant. A succession of persons had lain upon one or other of the three tressel-beds left vacant by Gavaudun, Sommarel, and Tourret; a strange procession of beings emblematical of the times: esurient lawyers from the provinces; disfrocked *abbés* much given to cards; Jews come to deal, if it might be, in assignats and the *domaines nationaux*. Nor were the lighter occupations of life unrepresented in these grim times. Not long since three players from the Théâtre de Lyons had been his room-fellows. One of them had got an engagement at the Théâtre Français in the Rue de Bondi; the other two had come up to bear him company, and look out for work and play. The last co-occupant of the room had called himself a composer. People said that he was in reality a Royalist agent, and he had been haled to the guillotine. Nay, but he was a composer, whatever else he might be; for his companion had one or two fragments of songs set to music by him which he had left behind in his hurry. Raynaud was now left in his ancient room alone; he himself was under the protection of Citizen Fourmisson, formerly barber, now member of the Tribunal Criminel Révolutionnaire, who lived in the better apartments below, and whose children Raynaud taught. But it was best to keep one's self to one's self in those suspicious days; and at that moment Raynaud reckoned not a single friend in Paris.

Life had not gone well with him. He was thinking this as, one winter afternoon, he returned to his room after giving his accustomed lesson on the floor below, and in spite of the cold stood for a moment gazing out from his window over the view of plots and cottages and distant woods which it showed. The houses and cottages had become more frequent, the patches of land fewer, during the last six years; for the faubourg had grown considerably. Raynaud noticed this much; he knew nothing about the changes in the rest of Paris. During the last three years he had never once crossed the river. He knew nothing of the changed appearance of the Quai de Grève since the conflagration, nothing of the new names which had been bestowed upon the parts of Paris near the Tuileries. Above all he had never been to the Place de la Révolution, nor seen the altar raised to the new patron saint of the City of Paris, la Sainte Guillotine. Certainly this indifference to the growth of the Republic, One and Indivisible, was in itself a thing suspect. But Citizen Fourmisson had his reasons for wishing to retain the services of the dreamy young tutor.

No; life had not gone well with him. Citizen Fourmisson paid his salary chiefly in the protection which his august name afforded. What Raynaud lived upon was a pittance due to him from his brother Gilbert, who cultivated the few patrimonial acres of Les Colombiers. 'Why do I linger on here?' Raynaud thought, or half-thought. 'What value is protection to a life so colourless as mine?" But then he realized that if he did talk of going, Fourmisson would without doubt denounce him at once. He thought of his last chamber-companion Briçonnet, the musician, the only one with whom he had made any sort of friendship; of the knocking which had mingled with Raynaud's dreams on that morning when the *sergents de ville* came to carry the poor composer off to the Luxembourg hard by; of the man's white face when he awoke, of how he had clutched at the bedstead and screamed to Raynaud to come to his help. The sergeants had searched everywhere, had ripped open the bed, but so far as Raynaud could see they had found nothing but scores of music. Most of the music they had carried away, but some scattered sheets remained. One contained the setting of a song by the unhappy Berthier de Saint Maur, who had been before then as little known to Raynaud as he was for long after to the English reader until, not long since, a critic unearthed him and translated some of his songs. It was a verse from the song of *Le Pèlerin* which was running in Raynaud's head now:

> Alone, alone, no mortal thing so much
> Alone! The eagle captured from the hills;
> The solitary *chouan** when he fills
> The air with discord; the cast mariner,
> What time the spar parts from his frozen clutch,
> Are not so lone as I,—ah no, sweet sir!

Raynaud even tried to sing the tune, as he had heard Briçonnet sing it. Singing was not in his way; he got nowhere near the air; rather the words came out in an unearthly chant.

Then, suddenly, he was brought back to the scene in this very room, six years before, when he and the three others had chanted together a magic formula out of a book by,—by,—he forgot the name. The whole scene rose before his eyes; then faded as quickly. No; his life had not gone well since then. He had in those ambitious student days (he had always passed then for the cleverest of the four) planned that great work on the *Comité des Nations*, an extension of the doctrine of the social contract into the domain of national law. It was to inaugurate a new era. The plan of the book and its very name were identical with those of the work which Gavaudun had actually published in these years; and which even in the times in which they lived had made him famous. Had Gavaudun taken his idea? Had he, Raynaud, left much on record? Had he expounded it fully in those days? He could not remember now; but he thought he had drawn it all out later. Yet it could not be so; Gavaudun must have stolen the thought from him. But his spirits felt too dulled to allow of his feeling active resentment even for such a piece of plagiarism as that.

Then Tourret; that was stranger still. Tourret had acted out in real life what had been Raynaud's dream. He had almost from boyhood had that romance in his mind. How he was to be riding along the dangerous way where the main road to Tours branches off from the Orleans road, there where the disused water-mill peeps out from among the trees,—that mill was always thought to be a rendezvous for footpads; how he was to overhear the two men planning the seizure of an approaching vehicle, was to ride past them receiving a shot through his hat (he remembered all the details), was to meet the coach in which sat an old father and a beautiful young daughter, to ride up (in imminent danger again of being shot) and give them warning. Alas, too late, for here are the two upon us! But the old father fires, he, Raynaud, fires, and the two rogues fall. But what if more are coming? So he offers his own horse to the father, and the daughter rides on pillion behind, Raynaud and the coachman driving after at the best rate they can make. The result, the eternal gratitude of the father and his, Raynaud's ultimate marriage to the beautiful heiress. Such had been Raynaud's romance, elaborated in every detail. And three years ago it had fallen to Tourret actually to do this thing! The robbers from whom Tourret saved his future father-in law were not common highwaymen, but two from the terrible band of the *chauffeurs,* wherefore his heroism had been the greater. Tourret had married the heiress, and had, it was thought, at the beginning of the troubles found his way out of France to Switzerland.

No; not well. And last night he had dreamed that a great treasure had been found on the farm at Les Colombiers. The dream was so vivid that even after he woke he had been speculating what he should do with the money, what new life he should lead. But now that his thoughts had run back into their accustomed sombre channel he saw things in a different light. He professed to be an enlightened thinker; but no small measure of rustic superstition lingered in his mind. Dreaming of a treasure he knew was reckoned a bad omen. Who knows what it might portend?

Musing of all these things Raynaud descended to take his walk. As he passed along the passage at the bottom of the house the *concierge* stopped him with the familiar and, as we should call it, insolent action which one citizen used to another in those days, and always emphasized if he had to do with a man better born and better educated than himself.

'A despatch for you, citizen,' he said.

The lower floor of this old hotel was now a wine-shop, and the two or three men in the room were grouped together examining a rather official-looking envelope bound round with a cord and sealed with black wax.

'Here is the citizen for the letter,' said the *concierge*; and the man who was actually holding it handed the envelope to the porter without apology and without rising. 'Good luck to the citizen with his letter,' he said, turning back to the table to take up his glass.

The others laughed a little, and all eyed Raynaud rather curiously as he broke the seals. The idea of Government was in those days almost synonymous with the idea of Death. Therefore even an envelope with an official seal upon it, especially if the seal were black, suggested the vague possibility either that the citizen who received it was going to be guillotined himself, or else that one of his relatives had been—not here in Paris, perhaps, but down in the country.

Raynaud with the thoughts that had been running in his head could not help turning pale as he opened the letter. But it proved to be of a very inoffensive character, though for some reason the Bureau of Police had thought fit to open and read it and seal it up again in this official manner. It was from Raynaud's brother Gilbert. 'My dear brother,' he wrote. 'The agriculture marches very ill here, no doubt in great measure because of the plots of Pitt and of the enemies of the Republic; but also because the workmen work not very willingly and there are not enough *métayers** to be found. It has happened that my brother-in-law Emile Plaidoyer has lately died. Wherefore my father-in law writes to offer me to work with him upon his farm of Guibrauche in Plessis-le-Pèlerin, where he prospers better than I. Now precisely at this moment comes an offer from Maistre Sommarel of Tours to buy Les Colombiers. He offers a good price for it, seven thousand livres. Wherefore if thou consent, my dear brother, the bargain shall be made and the instruments drawn up. D. G. Thy brother, Gilbert.' D. G. was the nearest that those who still possessed religion dared put for the ordinary salutation, *Dieu te garde.*

Curious; Raynaud's dream of last night come true, after a fashion! Only unhappily the treasure of which the dream spoke was diminished to this miserable sum of seven thousand livres, of which only the moiety would come to him. That at any rate was worth having. To-morrow he would write to Gilbert authorizing him to complete the sale. With that he issued into the street.

III

There was very little variety in Raynaud's walks. They took place at the same time, that is at the completion of his afternoon's lessons with his pupils, and therefore at this winter season just about the hour of dusk. They never extended outside a short radius from his lodging, and generally comprised some sort of a circle round Mount St. Geneviève. Up the Rue des Postes, the Rue Neuve St. Geneviève, down the Rue Mouf-fetard, the Rue Bordet, till he reached the Place du Panthéon; this was his route to-day. He extracted a certain dull pleasure from the sight of these familiar streets growing dusky in the gathering night. They made an image for him of the fading of all things, all worldly ambitions and troubles into the same dull twilight of the tomb; an image or half-image, for his thoughts themselves had grown dim and as it were muffled in his brain.

But to-night he was roused up a little, cheered by the letter which he had got from Gilbert. 'Maistre Sommarel, Som-marel,' he said to himself, as he reviewed the letter in his mind. 'Likely enough that is my old comrade Sommarel. He was a Tourrainais like myself; I know that. Everything seems to bring back those days to me this evening.' The scene of their last Christmas Eve came once more distinctly before his mind. 'And, *par Dieu!*' he thought to himself, 'if this is not also Christ-mas Eve!' The Christian religion had been abolished, and the months and the days of the month had been changed; so that it took Raynaud a minute to remember that this, the fourth of Nivose, was in 'slave-style' the twenty-fourth of December. But, as he walked, the words of the old incantation came back to him, and under his breath he kept on humming, to the self-same chant that they had used, the meaningless invocation,— 'Ja, Pa, Asmodai, Aleph, Beleph, Adonai, Gormo, Mormo, Sadaï!' It was sad nonsense.

At this moment, he was passing along the little street of St. Étienne des Grès, near the church of that name. He vaguely remembered that some years before some antiquarian studies which he had been making on pre-Roman Paris and its neigh-bourhood had given him a special interest in the site of this little church of St. Étienne; and that he had always meant to go into it, but had never done so. Since then he had forgotten his wish. He had no doubt passed the insignificant building a hundred times in his walks, but had never thought of enter-ing. Religion had now been abolished, and the churches were all closed. Raynaud presumed so at least, but he thought he might at any rate try this one. He found to his surprise that the handle would turn,—after an effort, rustily. The door swung complainingly open and he went in.

The place had not been used for a year. It was colder than the tomb. Spiders and dust in partnership had hung ropes from pillar to pillar; rats had been busy with the woodwork; a bat or two had found its way through a broken pane in the windows and built nests in the organ-loft and the rood-screen: Raynaud walked forward toward the apse in whose windows the light was beginning to fade. What a pity that he had not happened to have looked up his old notes, so as to know why he had once specially wished to stand inside this church of St. Étienne des Grès. But how curious that he should have so utterly forgotten those antiquarian studies of three years gone, and that they should come back to him now. Quite a flood of things seemed to be coming back to him. Was he in a dream now, or had he been in one through these last three years? Only give him time and he would remember everything.

'I am,' it said.

It said—what said? Raynaud could have sworn that no one spoke. And yet there again, 'I am and I was;' and it was as if the air laughed silently. 'Who are you?' he cried. But there was no answer, and he expected none. For he knew that he had heard no sound.

Then he gave a sudden start, and his heart beat against his ribs, and the sweat gathered on his forehead. For almost as if in answer to his invocation there came a sound from far off, a sound of footsteps drawing nearer and nearer. Raynaud cowered down, suddenly unnerved; and yet there was nothing supernatural in what he heard. The steps came nearer and nearer, and a crowd of men and women (passing by chance that way from a day spent in the Place de la Révolution) burst into the church,—figures not to be seen to-day save in a nightmare: haggard, long-toothed women with black hair or grey, tangled and lank, streaming down beside their cheeks; blear-eyed men, drunk, not with wine, but with a new intoxication to which men had not yet given a name, the intoxication of blood. They had come that way by chance, and seeing the church-door open had run in. But as they advanced up the aisle their step changed into a dance. They caught hold of one another and danced up the aisle, up to the chancel, up to the altar itself, throwing up their feet, their arms, clasping one another, whirling and whirling round. They shook the rood-screen, shook down ropes of cobwebs from the high roof, shook the organ loft, till the organ itself emitted a dull sound, half-groan, half-wail. Then they danced out, and silence, as ghost-like as before, fell on the deserted church. But the dance which had seized upon them there went with them out into the street. It was caught up by others and grew, and grew into a wild infection, a Dance of Death. It was called the Carmagnole.*

Raynaud was left once more alone. And again the Air spake: 'Swaying and whirling,' it said, 'whirling and swaying;' and then again, 'I did it;' and once again the Silence laughed.

Raynaud could bear it no longer, and he cried out in a tone which surprised even himself,—'Speak! Who are you? I command you to speak!' But there was no answer.

Then it was as if a wind blew through the church, and, yes, Raynaud heard the rustling of boughs above, and it seemed as if the moon were struggling to shine through branches far overhead. It was but a momentary vision; again he was alone in the church, and grey evening was changing into night.

'Ye Spirits of the Earth,' said Raynaud half mechanically, as the old conjuration came into his head; 'I call and conjure you! Be ye my aiders and confederates, and fulfil whatsoever I demand!'

'I am and I was,' said the voiceless Voice, and laughed again. But Raynaud no longer wondered what it meant, for the voice was within him.

IV

In the morning, long before dawn, Raynaud left his lodging. The porter was nodding by the door, and one man was asleep in the wine-shop with his head upon the table and a candle guttering in its iron saucer close beside him, sending forth much smoke and an evil smell. Raynaud undid the fastenings of the door softly and stole out. A bitter wind met him; some moist snow was lying thinly between the cobble-stones, and a few flakes were still falling. He passed with quick footsteps down the echoing Rue des Postes into the Rue St. Jacques, down and down, to places he had not trodden for years, over the Petit Pont into the Cité, and thence to the north side of the river. It was years since he had been there, and many things were new to him. The Quai de la Grève had been reconstructed since the conflagration; the last building on the Petit Pont had fallen. But Raynaud paid little heed to these things, nor yet to the river which he had not seen for so long, nor to the numberless barges laden chiefly with wood which lay upon the stream, nor the piles of wood all along its southern bank. From the Quai de la Grève he passed along the Quai de la Mégisserie, then along the Quai du Louvre, the Quai des Tuileries, until finally the Quai du Conférence brought him to the goal of his steps, the Place de la Révolution.

The Place was never free from loiterers night or day. Bitter as was the morning many were there now, sitting upon the steps which led up to the terrace of the Tuileries. In the faint moonlight they looked more like black shadows than men. For a moon far gone in the wane gleamed faintly over the trees to the north of the Place. And now, from where Raynaud paused for a moment to look about him, an object which he had never seen before stood between him and the moon, a square open scaffolding mounted upon a sort of rostrum. It was the guillotine! All round the rostrum hung a little group of men.

There were some guards between them and the erection itself, but not many, and they did not exercise their authority with much vigour to keep men from perching themselves upon the lower posts and under the bars of the construction. Raynaud without further pause pushed straight for this crowd, and tried to elbow his way as near as might be to the guillotine. His dress was undistinguished from that of any other member of the crowd. He wore a rough black coat of a sort of shag or frieze, black breeches of the same material. His waistcoat was red, with a blue and white stripe across it; his feet were shod with *sabots,*⋆ and he wore a red cotton nightcap on his head. That was the safest dress for any man to wear in those times. When however Raynaud set to work to elbow his way too pertinaciously to a good place near the guillotine, the crowd began to murmur, and as their eyes lighted upon his delicate white hands they began to bandy jests upon him in which an ear accustomed to the times would have recognized danger.

'It is well to be a good patriot, citizen,' said a little man standing beside a large fat woman; 'but let others be good patriots too.' ''*Cré nom, oui,*' growled another. 'Some come to *la mère* for one thing, some for another,' said the fat woman enigmatically. 'The citizen has not come expecting to meet a friend, *par exemple?*' said a fourth speaker, setting himself directly in Raynaud's way. 'Not a *ci-devant,*⋆ for instance?' 'Not come to pay respects to the head of his family?' '*Ou bien à la chef de la chef de sa famille,*' said a dullard, thinking that he had seen the pun for the first time and laughing heavily at his own wit. '*Bon jour, monsieur! monsieur!! monsieur!!!*' cried many voices in which shrill ones predominated, after Raynaud, who despite of all, and apparently not knowing what was said to him, had pushed and squeezed his way some yards nearer the machine, he was just at the corner of the scaffold. He contrived to settle himself on one of its under-beams in a sort of squatting attitude which rested him a little, and there he remained quiet and awaited the day. Some of the citizens who had joined in the gibes upon him continued for a while to growl threateningly.

Then something else attracted their attention and they left him in peace.

It was bitterly cold, though nobody seemed very sensible of it. Now and then flakes of snow still drifted lazily through the air. The moonlight faded in the sky, and the grey sad face of dawn began to look forth through the curtains of the east. At last she blushed a little; and between two black bars, like the bars of a prison-window, the sun himself shot a beam or two across the world.

By this time the Place de la Révolution was densely packed. Almost immediately after the sunrise there arose from all the mass a great sigh of satisfaction which shaped itself into the words '*On vient—on vient*—they are coming!' Then a regiment of soldiers marched up and formed round the scaffold. The crowd swayed backward, crushing and swearing. Raynaud seemed to be unaware of what was going on till a soldier rather roughly pulled him from his seat and threw him forward into the crowd. The people, who had jeered at him before, laughed and began to jeer at him again. But now a cruel sound was heard in the distance, the roar of an angry multitude. The excitement round the guillotine grew keener every moment; people pushed and swore and tried to raise themselves above their neighbours. One tall man who held a six-year-old child upon his shoulders was very conspicuous.

At the first sound of the distant roar Raynaud had raised his head; an eager light shone in his eyes as if he was listening to catch some definite words, and presently his own mouth opened and gave forth in a monotonous chant the old invocation: 'Ja, Pa, Adonai, Aleph, Beleph, Asmodai. . . .'

'What is he saying? He is mad,' said the citizens immediately round him, eyeing him askance. 'He is giving a signal; it is a plot,' said another. His life at that moment hung upon a thread; but he wist not of it.

The roar had been deepening all this time. Every throat in the Place de la Révolution began to take up the cries, which had been running like flame down the streets and quays. '*A bas les tyrans!'* was the usual cry, alternating here and there with *'Vive la guillotine!' 'Vive la République!'* Some people gave a lyrical turn to the noise by chanting a stanza of the Marseillaise—*'Aux armes, citoyens! . . .'*

The first tumbril reached the scaffold, which the executioner mounted the moment after, greeted by vehement cries of *'Vive Samson!'* and the process of reading out the names began, which to any one but those quite close to the performers seemed like an inexplicable dumb show. With his eyes almost bursting from his head with wild excitement Raynaud pushed and squeezed and sweated to get nearer still to the fatal engine. For now the first bound figure was brought forward and laid face downward upon the block. Suddenly the noise in the crowd died down, and men held their breaths to watch the final act of this man's life-comedy. There was always a special interest felt in the first execution of each day. Men made bets upon it; whether the head would leap off straight into the sack, or whether it would just touch the woodwork first, and so forth. What is stranger still, the superstitious drew auguries from this event; as if the world (which in the Place de la Révolution it had done) had rolled two thousand years backward in its course.

Raynaud was one of the very few in the crowd who beheld an execution for the first time. His heart stood still, but not with fear, to wait for the sound of the descending steel. And then—then it came. Men spoke often in those days of the executed man sneezing in the sack of sawdust. It was not merely a fanciful metaphor. The truth is that the sound which Raynaud's ears now heard for the first time had some grim resemblance to a sneeze. It was made partly by the swift hiss of the descending steel, checked for a moment as it shore through the victim's neck, partly by the head falling into the sack of sawdust, partly by the gush of the blood rushing forth when the head was severed. Such was the sound which followed the moment's pause of the listening crowd, and which Raynaud heard for the first time. And as he heard it the blood

coursed again through his veins, his eye glistened with a pre-
ternatural brightness, and he seemed to drink in new life.

The day wore on; Raynaud had eaten nothing since the
previous night, but he seemed to feel no hunger. One after
another the tumbrils discharged their burdens and the
bloody sacrifice went on. Sacrifice! yes, that was the word
which flashed into his mind. A sacrifice to whom or what? An
answer to that too seemed to lie somewhere in the back of his
thoughts, but he could not seize it then. The crowd around
him, which had been formerly so suspicious, could not help
being struck by his look of exultation, and repented itself of
its suspicions. And one man, who had not been noticed before,
with a dark face and a peculiarly acute cast of countenance,
was so pleased that he placed his hand on Raynaud's shoulder
with the usual compliment, 'I see you are a good patriot, citizen!'

At length the last cart had been emptied and a blank-
ness fell over Raynaud's soul. It was again dark. Quickly the
crowd began to disperse, not without wild cries and fraternal embraces and dancing of the new *carmagnole*. The acute
faced man came up and spoke to Raynaud, who listened as
if he understood, but understood nothing. The other gave
him a piece of his bread and a fragment of sausage. Then they
nodded and exchanged 'good-night,' and Raynaud walked
away.

V

Raynaud passed again along the quays and over the Petit
Pont toward his home. Suddenly he found himself once more
in the little church of St. Étienne des Grès. The day had been
long gone, and it was colder than ever. But the night was clear,
and the starlight stole in, muffled and shadowy, through the
east window of the church.

Through the east window,—but why did the groining of
the window seem to shake and sway from side to side? Why

did the air blow so cold through the church? There was an answer to this, Raynaud knew, but could not lay hold of it. From the organ-loft (if it was an organ-loft) came a sad sound like that which the wind makes through pine trees. Raynaud looked and looked into the recesses—of what?—the church? Nay; but they stretched far beyond the limits of the church. It was as if he were in the midst of a vast forest. Dim star-lit stems seemed to catch his eye from far distances girt round by shadow; and now over his head boughs were certainly waving to and fro.

Then a wild sort of half-chant filled his ears, wild but very faint. He could dimly fancy he caught the voices of his old comrades, Gavaudun, Sommarel, Tourret, in it; at any rate the chant brought them in some way into his mind. And the sound grew nearer and nearer, wilder and harsher. Figures came in sight, fierce in gesture, with unkempt locks streaming down their faces, clad in skins, brandishing spears on high, marching or dancing forward in a strange dance. Then there was a crashing among the branches and heavy-wheeled carts rumbled into sight, each drawn by two bullocks. Beside them walked men in white apparel, with fillets* round their hair. The carts were full of men and women, who all had their hands bound behind them, in some cases bound so tightly that the withes had cut through the flesh and a streak of blood trickled downward over their hands. Some opened their mouths from time to time, but whether to sigh or cry out Raynaud could not tell, for the shouting and screaming of the crowd would have drowned their voices. And now, as each cart came to the stopping place, the bound men were one by one brought down, a white-robed priest plunged a knife into each one's cart, and the blood flowed out upon the ground. The cries and chanting grew louder and louder; people danced in ecstasy round the pool of blood, which was swelling almost into a rivulet, and flowed away among the trees. Then, as suddenly as it had begun, it all ceased; and Raynaud saw the dark church round him with a faint light struggling in through the window. And within him the silent Voice spoke,—'I am the spirit of the place. I did it. Two thousand years ago, and yesterday and—' Thereupon the whole air seemed to be filled with pale faces of slaughtered victims, who moved round as in a procession. Raynaud saw at last the faces of his three old comrades of the Rue Pot-de-Fer following one after the other, and at the end of all a fourth face,—his own!

VI

He returned to his lodging. Citoyenne Fourmisson met him on his way to his room, and poured upon him a torrent of abuse and threats. But he only stared at her and passed on. What had that past life to do with him now? The world had begun to live anew, and all the new life was coursing through his veins. Fourmisson was away; he had been sent with Tallien to sharpen the sword of the Revolutionary Committee at Bordeaux and stamp out the last embers of Girondinism.

The next morning, and the next, and the next, Raynaud was in his old place beside the scaffolding of the guillotine. Each day he encountered his friend of the first occasion; sometimes these two walked part of the way home together. The acute-faced one was full of statistics: of how many could be executed by one 'machinist' in a single day; of what work had been done by a rival machine in the Champ de Mars; of work that was being done in the provinces. One evening, after a modest dinner together, he took Raynaud into another church he had never been in before. It too was in the neighbourhood of Mont de Geneviève. It was a huge church this, not like that of St. Étienne de Grès disused and empty, but crammed with—worshippers shall we say!—yes, worshippers of a sort. The same wild feeling of exultation that he had felt first in St. Étienne and again by the guillotine, seized the student now, as he came among these cloisters and looked along the sea of red caps and dark unwashed faces which the place contained. Many were smoking; a hot thick atmosphere rose from the standing throng, and behind it danced a sea of faces which crowded the amphitheatre of benches in the nave and reached almost to the roof of the church. Raynaud had seen long since a print from some picture by an Italian master in which tiers and tiers of angels, all bearing instruments of music in their hands, rose one above the other as to the roof of heaven. These were not the faces of angels; nor was it like sweet music the sound which came from their throats when the speaker in a high tribune paused in his oration. This place was the debating-hall of the Société des Amis de la Liberté; and the church was the church of the Convent of the Jacobins.

As his friend spoke to this man and that, helping him forward, Raynaud felt the last traces of his old dulness and indifference fall off him like a cast garment. The whole assembly was but an instrument to be played upon—and a vision of the rat-riddled organ of St. Étienne flashed through his mind; he would make it sound what tune he chose. He was not therefore the least surprised to find himself presently in the tribune. The motion before the society was not of much importance, merely one for the expulsion of one Legrand who, his enemies pointed out, had been once the signatory of an *arrêt* in favour of the 'traitor' Lafayette. Such an act of expulsion would have been of course only the first stage on the road to the guillotine; but in the case of a single individual, of what consequence was that? What Raynaud said upon the motion was, like most of the other speeches, pretty wide of the subject in hand. But his peroration stirred the audience to frenzy. 'Our duty,' he cried, and it was as if a sonorous voice not his own had been lodged within him, 'our duty, the duty of France, is to purify the whole world; and that can only be done by blood, and more blood, by blood ever and always!' And when he ended, the human organ round him swelled into such a diapason of rough-throated applause as had never been heard in that church before.

Raynaud became a celebrity. He was placed upon the Revolutionary Committee, and the work of that body went forward ever more rapidly under the inspiration of his zeal. He seemed to require no rest nor food, and whenever he was not occupied upon the tribunal he was sure to be seen in a cart by the guillotine, or on the scaffold itself, superintending the execution of its victims. In those days he carried a motion that the sittings of his tribunal should not begin till the afternoon, but should be prolonged, if needful, into the night; for the work of Samson and his colleagues was generally over before four. Great was the increase in the rapidity of work at the tribunals, and the growth of the *fournées*,—the batches of men who wended daily to the Place. It was through the motion of Raynaud that eventually a third guillotine was set up at the edge of the Faubourg St. Marcel, on his side of the river, nearer still to that site of the old grove of sacrifice where now stood St. Étienne des Grès.

But there were days of pause. On the *decadis,* for example, the present substitutes for Sunday, no work was done; no prisoners were executed on that day. And on such days Raynaud would sit quietly at home over his books, the gentlest citizen in Paris. He would allow no suitors to him on that day, for his readings were deep. He had found his old volume of John of Menz, and read much in him in those days. On one of these *decadis* (it happened to be a Sunday also, if such things had been taken account of) he was sitting thus occupied in his old room when a messenger did gain admittance, bringing a note. Raynaud gave a start of pleasure as he read it. It was signed 'Sommarel,' and it asked him to go and see the writer, who, it seemed, was in the prison of La Force. A pleasant air of ancient days seemed to breathe round Raynaud as he read the old handwriting and saw the familiar name. He put down his book and followed the messenger at once.

Sommarel came to meet him, white and trembling, very dirty too, though his clothes were better than those which the citizens of Paris thought it wise to wear. He had an ugly cut upon his cheek, which showed purple against his dead white skin.

'I never knew anything about it when I bought the prop-
erty,' he began at once, almost before Raynaud had had time
to greet him, and his voice trembled miserably. 'God is my
witness, monsieur, that I never knew! I was preparing to write
to monsieur, to the illustrious citizen, and tell him—Ah, *mon
Dieu*, citizen, my old friend, save me, save me! I have a wife
and—' and here his trembling voice broke into sobs.

'*Dieu de Dieu*, what does he mean?' said Raynaud, in his
gentle voice. 'What is it, my old comrade? You are beside your-
self.'

'What? The money, the treasure that I found,—was I not
arrested because of that?' Sommarel checked himself in his
explanation. His voice trembled less.

'Money? Treasure? I know nothing of it,' Raynaud said
dreamily, passing his hand before his face. 'Treasure? Ah, at
Les Colombiers? I heard something of that,—long ago,' he
added, as if plunged in a deep reverie.

Sommarel stared. He had only completed the purchase
of Les Colombiers two months previously, and it was only a
week since he had discovered under an old apple tree an iron
box containing three thousand pieces of twenty livres,—sixty
thousand livres in gold, besides jewels. He had thought of
making some communication to Raynaud, who was too pow-
erful a person to be left unpropitiated; but had taken no steps
toward doing so till three days before he had been arrested
and carried up to Paris. If he had only waited and not been
so unnerved by fear! He tried now to put a good face upon it.
'Ah, then my arrest had been no doubt a pure mistake. How
fortunate that you, my old friend, should have the power of
releasing me so easily! You will order me to be set at liberty at
once, *n'est-ce pas?*'

Raynaud's face darkened. It was as if some subject totally
foreign to his present thoughts had been forced upon him. 'I
have not the power,' he said briefly; and while that dark look
was on his face Sommarel dared not press the point.

Presently his face cleared, and he and his old comrade

exchanged information about their lives since the day when they parted close upon six years ago.

Sommarel had prospered moderately (he was careful to say only moderately) as a lawyer in Tours, had taken to himself a wife, and had two children. He looked piteously up at Raynaud as he told him these last details. But the other only went on to ask about Tourret and Gavaudun. Tourret, it seemed, had not gone to Switzerland. His father-in-law, the *ci-devant*, was dead. Tourret and his wife had still a moderate income, and lived quietly in Auvergne. During all the talk Sommarel watched (as a dog watches) the face of his friend. He had, Sommarel saw, the same mild dreamy eyes which the young student had in days of yore, the same gentle voice. At last Raynaud got up to go.

'Ah! *mon Dieu*, Geoffroi, thou wilt not leave me here. Consider the danger! Have pity, have pity; think of my wife, my children!' Again his voice was choked with fear and grief.

Once more the dark look came into Raynaud's face. 'I have not the power,' he said, and hurried out.

Sommarel was in one of the early batches that came up for trial. But as a matter of fact his arrest had been a mistake, and there really appeared to be nothing against him. The Tribunal however hesitated to acquit; acquitting was an act which seemed almost contrary to nature. Besides this lawyer of Tours wore a better coat and finer linen than seemed compatible with the best citizenship,—always excepting the case of Robespierre, who was allowed by public opinion to wear silk stockings and gilt buckles. Still you could not precisely condemn a man for wearing good clothes. 'What do you think?' one member whispered to Raynaud. 'Must one acquit?' Raynaud made no answer; he only stepped from his seat on the rostrum to the body of the hall.

'I denounce the citizen,' he said. 'I have known him long, and I know him a proper subject for the guillotine.'

'Geoffroi, my friend, have pity on me!' was all that Sommarel could say.

'Ah,' said the other members, 'he acknowledges the old acquaintanceship. Citizen Raynaud has acted the part of a good patriot!' And Sommarel was removed.

VII

Everybody spoke of this act of patriotism on the part of Raynaud. It had its imitators; and before long it came to be a distinguishing note of Roman virtue to denounce some relative or friend. In such a case denunciation meant death as a matter of course. It was argued that only under the pressure of the most ardent patriotism had private feelings been so far sacrificed. To question therefore the knowledge of one who had been wrought to such a step was clearly absurd.

To Raynaud it only meant that the batches grew larger day by day. There was a question of dividing the Revolutionary Tribunal that the work of trial might be more expeditious, and Raynaud warmly advocated the scheme. Robespierre advocated it too. There were found some who said the gentle-eyed author of the saying, *Il faut du sang, et encore du sang, et toujours du sang,* was a better patriot than Robespierre himself; so Robespierre coldly advocated the scheme for division of the Tribunals and it was carried.

On the other hand the friends of Robespierre remarked that though it was Raynaud who had set the fashion of 'denouncings,' and though it was he who had finally introduced the practice of accepting these denouncings in the place of evidence, no more of his own friends or relations ever appeared before the Tribunals. The discontent which these hints began to arouse went so far that at last one of the denounced ones was acquitted by Raynaud's own Tribunal against his earnest pleadings. Of late, moreover, Samson had once been hissed and not cheered when he mounted the guillotine in the Place de la Révolution, and the tumbrils were no longer cursed so loudly as they rolled through the streets. No crowds preceded them dancing the *carmagnole* and singing; on the contrary, the crowd sometimes stood silent, some women were even heard to use words of pity. Raynaud himself witnessed this scene; he went home and took to his bed. Robespierre was said to have declared that he was going too far and demoralizing the guillotine.

Should he denounce his brother Gilbert and so vindicate his position once more? There was Tourret too living in Auvergne. Yes, he decided on both these; anything must be done rather than that the daily sacrifice should grow less. Meantime a piece of good fortune happened. Gavaudun, teaching French literature and law in Prague, had heard that Raynaud had risen to a position of importance without hearing of the details. He wrote to his former comrade asking for some help in a matter of private interest. Raynaud replied and succeeded at length in enticing Gavaudun to an interview with a supposed notary and notary's clerk upon the Swiss frontier. Gavaudun was seized and carried to Paris, denounced and executed. Raynaud's influence rose again: the batch of *condamnés* next day increased from thirty-nine to sixty-three; and once more the blood seemed to course through his veins.

But alas! next day came the news that Gilbert Raynaud had escaped. Only his father-in-law, old Plaidoyer, was seized. And people began to murmur against Raynaud again. But then Tourret had been taken; so came the news the day following; and he in due course was brought up to Paris.

It was said that seldom had a prisoner pleaded more eloquently than Tourret did. His speech was delivered as though addressed personally to Raynaud and to him alone, though in fact the latter was not holding the position of a judge but of a witness. Tourret spoke of their old comradeship, of pleasures and hardships shared in common, of this act of kindness on the part of Raynaud, of that return by himself. Then he went on to plead the innocence of his life since, buried as he had been down in the country,—'simple-minded and avoiding State affairs,' as he said, quoting in Greek; for he and Raynaud had read Aristophanes together in the old days. A momentary

smile flitted across Raynaud's unexpressive face as he heard
these words; for he knew that if there had been any disposition
to acquit upon the part of the judges, this display of learning
would probably just turn the scale. Tourret went on to speak
of his father-in-law lately dead, of his wife and one child, and
his voice faltered a little—not overmuch. He spoke like a born
orator; even the judges were moved; and Citizen Fourmisson whispered, looking at Raynaud's impassive countenance,
'That man has a heart of stone.' But then Citizen Fourmisson
had always been of the party secretly opposed to the Aristides
of the Tribunal. Aristides himself was as one who only listened for form's sake. When the speech was over he raised his
head with that peculiar light in his eyes which seemed almost
to mesmerize his fellow-judges and to call forth the word he
expected. *Condamné!* came from all mouths at once, and the
prisoner was removed to make way for the next.

VIII

Of the next day's batch to the guillotine in the Faubourg St.
Marcel Tourret was the first name on the list. Raynaud was,
as usual, upon the platform. Robespierre too had come that
day to assist at the executions, jealous of the other's growing
reputation for patriotism of an exalted kind. There were one
or two other citizens of some note there. But these two stood
before the rest, the observed of all observers; Robespierre at
any rate was, for he was not often seen in that remote south-
east region. He had on an elegant drab coat, black breeches,
and white stockings. Raynaud was in his usual coarse black
coat and breeches and red cap of liberty; and out of these
rough habiliments the singular delicacy of his features, the singular long white hands, showed only the more conspicuous.

He watched the cart as it drew up to the scaffold, watched
the victims while they answered to their names, watched the
first of them, Tourret, as he was brought upon the platform
bound,—yet not as if he had ever seen him before, though

his comrade cast upon him a glance which might have awed a Judas,—watched him as he was led forward and placed with his head upon the block.

There was, it has been said, always a momentary pause and hush before the fall of the first head. The details of the performance this day were the same as on the previous one. The swift-checked hiss, a dull,—a very dull thud.

Then a woman screamed as never woman had screamed before. The sound sent a thrill of horror through even that crowd, used as it was to horrors of many kinds. Those who were a little way off set the woman down as the wife of the condemned. But those who were close to her saw that she had not even been looking at the victim, that her eyes had been fixed upon Robespierre and his com—

But there was nobody standing beside Robespierre!

The woman was foaming at the mouth. '*Mon Dieu, c'était le diable!*' she moaned. Samson had hold of the head; he turned to display it first to the two great men. Robespierre on his part turned round to speak to his neighbour, and then his face grew white to the lips. There was no Raynaud beside him! Others had seen the same sight that the woman had seen. 'It was Robespierre's familiar spirit,' they said; and in the talk which grew out of what they had to tell lay the germ of Thermidor.*

But one acute-faced man close to the scaffolding was heard to murmur, 'The mystic chain is broken—*Catena mystica rupta est!*'

PHANTASIES

I—THE ALP WANDERER

THE fir-trees pointed their heads to heaven, funereal giants and, to me, a mortal seemed to touch the stars. From above, other fir-trees looked down upon their summits, which from that height were flattened upon the lower branches, and altogether appeared spread out like fungi or lichens upon the earth. Above the highest of the high trees the bare rock began to climb, until it was hidden by the feet of the glacier. But the glacier's head pillowed and lost itself upon eternal snows. From these snows the glacier, the rocks, the fir-crowned hills, the dark valley beneath, which murmured with innumerable waters, were as nought, terrene things of no account to those eternal witnesses.

The snow-fields were swept by the skirts of the cloud, rainbow-tinted at the edges, and between these looked on them the face of the moon as the face of a friend.

Below on earth mortal men praised her and appeased her with nameless sacrifices. She moved unheeding, girt round by sombre night, spreading awful shadows through the midnight wood. The mandrake felt the touch of her beams and half unloosed its clinging root beneath the soil; dark hellebore matted itself in the thicket and gave forth its deadly odour. And Penthesilea, with fearful incantations, moved, now in the light, now in the blackness, gathering the herbs which were to serve her in her obscene rites while holy mortals slept.

But one man passed far above these things, too far for sight. He yet made, had there been any to behold him, a single dark stain upon the unapproachable whiteness of the snow. But his face, ever lifted towards the moon, showed the paleness of the planet; and in each of his eyes she saw herself.

To his fellows below he was a man distraught. The beings of the height, the storms which sat musing with ready wings in the clefts of the mountains, the avalanche which stood rapt poising a glittering spear watched him struggle on, and neither waved him back nor gave him welcome. Only the moon might seem to beckon him onward; for once she bowed her head through the veil edged with rainbow. The genii of the frost and snow looked at one another as he clambered onwards and mutely made him the sign of warning—might he but understand. Only on one condition may mortal men venture among these *demons* of the Alps.

The man distraught climbed up and up, for he thought that at the highest point he should see the moon unveiled and eye to eye.

And almost now had he begun the last ascent when the moon deepened her veil, and imposing black upon black she hid her face.

Then it seemed to the alp wanderer that she fled from him, and he cried aloud to the goddess. Below the mandrake under the hand of the witch gave forth the yell which draws men to madness. Penthesilea struck blood from her breast, and hellebore forgot to breathe into the darkened air.

Alas! At a sign the musing winds arose. With horrid cries they swept up with their wings white tornadoes which danced like witches in the chill air. Avalanche sprang from his peak, hurling his spear before him as he leapt. His white shaft struck the rash adventuring man.

The moon uncovered her face. No more did any stain of blackness mar the eternal snows. No more, for ever, did she behold her face reflected as but then in human eyes.

II—Destination

Those steps approaching and approaching along my dark

passage, wooden gallery call it, like the between decks of some huge old hull, wooden above, wooden on both sides, wooden beneath; how they echo! Always they draw nearer and nearer to my *atelier** door (why will they not make for one of the other studios?), yet never reaching it. No, never reaching it, though I should wait for them an hour. But there is no use in waiting. Anybody would know that they meant a summons. What the late tenant of my studio did when he heard them I need not guess. Did he ever hear them? or have they now come for the first time?

It was a winter afternoon, with even some attempts at sleeting; and already the shadows were beginning to collect in groups in the corners, in doorways. There was quite a regiment of them drawn up in the Rue de Grenelle.

It was in the Rue de Grenelle, which, except for the shadows, I had to myself, that I heard my own footsteps following and going in front of me all at once: even when I stopped they went on. The next thing I saw was a fat boy in a black *tablier** and a leathern belt crying by himself in an archway. After that I was not, of course, surprised, when I crossed over to look in at the armourer's in the Rue des Saints-Pères, to see in the midst of the Francis I shield in the window, instead of the gorgon's head which ought to have been there, my own face very neatly carved in bronze.

At the corner of the Rue de Rennes I found a conveyance without coachman or horses making its way up the street, so I got in. Now, a great number of years ago—I was returning from my first visit to France—I met in the train a fellow countryman in the fruit-dealing interest, whose business had taken him to the Channel Islands and Normandy, and his pleasure or adventure to Paris. As he knew scarce a word of the French he contrived, as he explained to me, this method of seeing the town: he mounted on the top of any public vehicle which was passing, and simply said the word *destination*, and so stayed undisturbed till he came to the journey's end. The sudden recollection of the fruit merchant suggested to me my course of procedure. Wherefore I had no sooner got inside the conveyance and shut the door behind me than I pronounced this word, *destination*, though, had I thought of it, there was neither driver nor conductor to pay attention to my wishes.

The word had some effect, however. For among the figures in the dark interior there went round a light titter, and I very distinctly heard some one say—though I cannot, in looking back, declare whether it was uttered in French or English—'Ah, yes, that is where we are all bound.'

The vehicle was not a large one, and was not lighted—at any rate not properly, for I could hardly see the persons I was close to. But it seemed to be almost choke-full. The only fellow travellers I did take note of were a man and a woman seated side by side at the top end. Not so much that I distinctly saw them as that, feeling a little ashamed, I think, of the titter which had gone round at my expense, they gave a slight apologetic bow in my direction, and I bowed back.

While I was taking in all these things at my leisure, we certainly ought to have arrived at the top of the Rue de Rennes. This, at least, I was momentarily expecting at first. I was too tightly wedged in to turn and look, and there must have been a thickish sleet or snow falling now, for the windows were encrusted by it. I saw no lights of shops or gas lamps. We had gone straight on. Surely by this time we should have arrived at the Montparnasse terminus? For you know that the Gare de Montparnasse shuts in all the southern end of the Place de Rennes, into which the Rue de Rennes debouches from the northern side. Or had we reversed a feat of a Western Railway locomotive not long since; and, as that jumped through one of the windows of Montparnasse Station into the Place, had we jumped from the latter into the Station, and got thence by rail into the open country?

Not by rail: that at least was clear. The jog-jog and grind-grind of the roadway were still beneath us. But were we going on for ever? Surely there were trees visible at the side; nay, by glimpses, what looked like a whole snowy landscape.

How cold it was! How thickly the snow coated the window panes! Now I think of it, it had been a mild, humid day until the time when I went out for a second while and found myself presently in the Rue de Grenelle. Well, in for a penny in for a pound! There was something inexpressibly fascinating in the suggestion of those high swaying trees, of that snowy landscape. Besides, was it not the night of St. Sylvester?

One reason why the conveyance was colder than it had been was that there were so much fewer people in it. Why I had not noticed this earlier I do not know. For, instinctively, I had taken advantage of the fact to wedge myself nearer and nearer the upper end of the car, away from the door. Wherefore now I was no distance from the old gentleman and lady who had first made a motion towards me. I say 'old': I judged them so from their figures, their faces I could hardly see. They seemed quite ready for me to speak to them, and I did so. Whether we talked in English or in French I vow I cannot recall.

We exchanged the usual banalities. Presently the old gentleman said: 'I was glad to see you get in—we were glad to see you get in.'

'Yes, indeed,' the lady assented, and gave a little sigh.

'It is so much more comfortable when people once make up their minds to do it.' This from her neighbour.

'O, as for that,' I said, 'there was no making up my mind in my case——'

'No, of course,' the man put in. 'That is a mere *façon de parler.*'*

'I got in by mere accident——'

'Yes, yes,' he interrupted again.

'And in the impulse of the moment.'

Once again I heard what I might call the ghost of a titter going round the carriage. But not, so far as I could detect, from either of my interlocutors. The man only gave a vague motion of assent.

'And I haven't a notion of how long I shall stay or where I am going to.'

'Chutch—chutch.' That certainly came from the old gentleman. There had been once more the thinnest ghost of a laugh from the other travellers.

'Yet I thought you mentioned the place?' he queried urbanely.

'The place? O—ah, yes. I said *Destination*. But that was only a—' 'joke' I had been going to say, and then to tell him the story of my Northumbrian fruit merchant. But somehow before I ever arrived at that word 'joke' I heard so distinctly, somewhere at the back of my head (for I will swear there was complete silence on behalf of my fellow passengers) the phrase 'O, yes: we all came here only for a joke': and at the end of the response the same laugh that I had already listened to three times, and which was beginning to grow disagreeable to me—I heard all these things, I say, so plainly by anticipation, that I stopped suddenly with my sentence unfinished.

Then the old lady for the first time opened the conversation. She seemed to be a rather sentimental personage with a tendency to sigh:—'It is so interesting that you should be travelling with us again.'

'Again?' I put in.

'Yes, it is indeed,' the man said, as speaking to his neighbour. And then, turning to me: 'And in my opinion it's greatly to your credit.'

'Of course I say the same,' the woman said.

Now we none of us like to disown a thing which is esteemed greatly to our credit. Still after a diplomatic hesitation truth, or curiosity, got the better of me. 'But I don't—I haven't the honour,' I was beginning.

'O come, come!' cried the man, 'you won't pretend you do not know my voice?'

'Well, I must confess its tones are familiar. But I couldn't add a name to them.'

'Do you go so far as to say you would not know me again?' And this time the man spoke with a hint of severity.

'Or me?' said the sentimental old lady in a slightly *espiègle** manner.

'Why, y—yes,' I stammered, 'I do know you if it comes to that. I—I know you quite well though you're changed. You are——'

'Your First Love and your First Ambition.' The two elderly people spoke almost in unison, and bowed towards me as they spoke.

Now, I confess that up to that moment, though the man I had been inclined to like from the first, I had been three parts disposed to think his companion some flighty middle-aged matron or maid. But the longer I looked at her kindly face, somewhat wrinkled though it was, and her serene blue eyes, the less and less was I ready to confirm my earlier judgment. Nay, before a minute had gone by I found a great rush of friendliness, not to say, tenderness, in my feelings towards both these two elderly creatures, who sat so bravely and uprightly side by side, and seemed to support the fatigues of the jolty convey-ance, the cold of the night, so well. For, though I was no longer acutely conscious of things outside, we must by now have got—how I cannot guess—far away into the bleak, open coun-try. I had a second consciousness of a great plain, such as are common enough in France. It was shrouded in snow, and the wind blew across it keenly; and everywhere ice was crunching in the streams and canals. I had a secondary consciousness of these things, though distinctly recognise them I could not. My first thoughts were all taken up by the two nearly opposite me, and in that sudden inrush of softness in the direction of both whereof I have spoken, I held out a hand to each. 'Now we *have* met once more,' I exclaimed heartily, 'we'll travel on to the—to the "destination."' 'But couldn't I,' I thought, 'get a seat right opposite you?' And I moved as if to go one place higher up.

'Hardly that!' I don't know to this day whether the man spoke in answer to my word or to my act. 'This seat is occu-pied,' he went on. And, indeed, the very while that he spoke I seemed to see a shadowy form in that last chair at the extreme end of the conveyance. The dim light or something else had prevented my seeing before that it was taken.

'You must present him,' the old lady said, and she sighed once again.

'Yes,' replied the man; and, though he spoke with a great show of cheerfulness, I fancied the tone was a thought forced. 'Yes, I must make you known to one another. This,'—and as he spoke he waved his hand towards the dim figure in the last chair—'is your *last* love and your *last* ambition. And his name is Père La Chaise.'*

III—THE PUPPET SHOW

'Well, they've put poor Gribble into his box.' He heard that in fancy as distinctly as with actual ears—spoken at his club, the Windham. And though he had not been previously notable for a sense of humour, this sentence made him almost burst with laughter.

'Into his box, that's just it! Such a delightful idea! Put your-self into a box like a toy.' It was the Thought at his Elbow which said that. But the testator laughed till he almost crowed at the notion.

To be a toy—the very summit of ambition. The most delightful thing imaginable, a toy among toys. 'A toy of the right sort,' said the Thought at his Elbow, 'such as that, for instance.' And, by Heaven, it was a toy of toys.

Who could have believed it was possible to make houses with such an exactitude in every detail as those which towered up, enclosing a paved court? Every stone, and a few chance blades of grass at one corner where a paving stone had been a little displaced; nay, almost down to the flakes of soot floating in the air; a thing of wonder. But after all this wonderful detail of the setting (so to call it) of the toy was as nothing compared to the thing when it began to work. For there came into it a perfect crowd of live manikins, almost all in black coats and shiny silk hats. They walked about, and formed themselves into little groups from two to three up to near a dozen. Some appeared laughing and joking: others extremely serious. The

most part had little pocket-books in which they were continu-
ally making entries, and a good number had printed sheets in
their hands, others unfolded newspapers. Then high up in one
window, which overlooked the court, Gribble could see a pale
woman working a type-writer. Higher up still, in an attic, was
an old creature trying to sew by the brown light.

'Or that,' said the Thought at his Elbow, after a good period
had gone by. And the second toy was not less wonderful than
the first. It represented a lighted drawing-room. The little elec-
tric lights in the centre of the ceiling, about as large as a pin-
head, were all countable. The manikins were men and women,
who walked about, moved their fans, blew their noses, twirled
with their watch-chains, and thrust pocket handkerchiefs up
their cuffs. And when Gribble had contemplated this for a long
time, he turned back to look at the first. And this time he saw
many things that had escaped him before.

'By all that's holy,' he cried, 'it's Capel Court! Why, and
that's Tommy Sneyd. Hang me, if it isn't!' Gribble used much
more moderate expressions than he had been wont to do formerly. 'That's Howard Jones; that's Cavendish Smith; there
goes White-White; there's . . .' and one by one he made out all
his old acquaintance.

Moreover, the manikins did not always repeat the same
action. Now one who had been looking into a newspaper,
would fold it up and join a group. From that group another
would separate, and go out of the court. And so on. It may
be fancied that the interest of watching all these changes was
not easily exhausted. And, when he did get a little satiated, he
turned back to the second toy. Here, again, it put on a new
character, for now he recognised acquaintance just as numerous here. 'The missis and Bella!' he cried with such delight,
and slapped his thigh so vigorously that the tears stood in his
eyes. For at last he had discovered his wife and daughter in the
room.

Now more alert, he at once recognised in a third toy the
card-room at the Windham, got absorbed in watching—for

he could count all the pips, though the cards were not a tenth the size of postage-stamps—the hand which Beresford-Budge was playing against White-White and Hartshill, and with the Colonel (of Volunteers).

Nor was this all. There were other manikin-toys just as interesting. 'One could go on looking at them for an eternity, couldn't one?' said the Thought at Gribble's elbow. Gribble was too much absorbed to answer that moment. But after a while, how long a while he could form no guess, he suddenly remembered that he had been spoken to. 'Well, not for an eternity, exactly,' he replied. But the Thought at his Elbow was no longer there.

'Not for ever,' at last said Gribble again, stretching himself a little as if preparatory to a yawn. It seemed to invite a remark from some one. But there was no answer. Certainly they were curious, these toys. He became absorbed once more for another period. But eventually he completed his yawn.

'It's about time this should stop,' Gribble said finally, turning away from a view of a country picnic. But that only brought him face to face with the card-room at the Windham. 'Jolly good time it should stop—for a bit. I'm da—hanged if it isn't.' But the shows went on.

At length a voice out of the Void explained things. 'You see,' it said, 'that—over there—you were not remarkable for a sense of humour, but you were distinguished by a marked business capacity. And business capacity consists, if you come to think of it, in treating your fellow creatures, not as if they were sentient beings, but as if they were puppets. The result is that the living beings who come here do not care to associate with you. We are trying to find what amusement we can for you. This is really the best we have to offer.'

Here Gribble lost his temper. 'How long, confound it, am I to go on looking at the infernal things?' he said, getting purple.

'You might be more polite. I said we were doing our best.'

'How long—that's what I want to know—*am* I to go on looking at the conf—the toys? It seems an age already since—'

'It is an age. It's exactly a hundred years.'

From purple Gribble turned ghastly pale. His teeth chattered. 'A hun—a hundred years! Good God! . . . And to—how long must I go on still?'

'Ah! That I can't say. Possibly for eternity. If so it can't be helped.'

'But look here, look here,' said Gribble. 'Tha—that's a—absurd, you know. L—look here, I just want to ask a question——'

No voice replied.

IV—A Possibility

It is an uncanny thing to have to grope your way into a cave, almost bent double, till you think the long mouth will never come to an end, and yet you must go on and on. For your spine feels so broken that you could not move backwards, and to turn round is a thing impossible.

Worse is to creep upon your belly along the entrance to a prehistoric fort of unhewn stones, and fancy that one of these huge slabs may dislodge and pin you there for ever.

But even this is not so bad as to be obliged to push forward in a smooth iron cylinder, which compresses arms and shoulders, back and chest, as a chicken is compressed in its egg. To know, too, that you *must* get through and emerge into the light—you cannot see the light, for your chin is bent upon your breast-bone—or abandon all hope! Yet this is just what the spirit of the dying man experienced, struggling and struggling to free itself from the body.

'I can quite understand,' it said to itself, 'the commiseration of the people who are standing round the bed (I would to Heaven I could get my head out, and then I should see them!). If they would only direct it to the proper quarter—— But it does seem absurd that they should give all their attention to the miserable shell that holds me in this manner, whereas of me myself they take no heed whatever. But I suppose not even my toes are sticking out the other end. Ugh! it's stifling. I'm jammed; there's no doubt about it. Come! one more wriggle. I believe I go back two inches for every one I get forward. It's the not being able to see ahead which is the worst part. Ugh! Courage! By—Jove!—I am getting—I'm *out!*

'And now, forsooth, they are going into tears and sobs! Was the like of it ever seen?

'I'm all in a sweat. But, by Heaven! as I said before, to be through with such a business! It was worth while for the mere pleasure of knowing that one was through.

'And the extraordinary lightness one feels!' the disembodied spirit went on presently. 'I feel as if I could fly out of the window straight away into space; though, of course, I know that's an impossibility.'

Yet, albeit the spirit remained in the death-chamber and close to its body, as it was bound to do; the mere sensation of utter immateriality, of a condition fitting one to fly clear away into space, was so intoxicating that it was not dull a moment.

It took no note of the flight of time, and a day or two passed over its disembodied head.

'Now my time is coming,' it found itself saying, with renewed assurance, one morning. 'I am beginning to move. I feel ten times as light and unsubstantial as I did even when I first got free from my fleshly envelope. What are these shapes moving about? What was that hammering noise I heard a while ago? I'm . . . . no longer in a room . . . . I've a notion that the sun is shining and a bird singing somewhere . . . . Is it the sun or the moon that I am under? I could almost fancy that I heard a tremendous shriek, such as I should have given if I saw a ghost . . . . But I cannot pay attention to such things . . . . now I'm growing lighter . . . . more spiritualised. . . . . My time is . . . . coming.'

But that was the last thought which passed through the—brain?—no; mind, shall I say?—of the disembodied spirit. For by now it had sucked out all the vital essence that remained in the corpse which it had left. And then it ceased to be.

V—THE PROFESSOR

The Professor sat gazing into his fire, a fire of glowing peat overlaid with logs, according to his special predilection. 'It is just the fire I like,' he said; 'and I can afford to treat myself to what I like now.'

A glow of self-satisfaction would have been inevitable in the circumstances, even to an Englishman. But this was a Scottish Professor, and the satisfaction was increased many times. 'And not only wood,' he went on to himself, 'but old ship's timber.'

In truth, it was a sight to see how the flames sprang up and talked and cackled and burned, now white, now red, now blue, now green, like the changing lights of a harbour; a thing to mark how the smoke pitched and plunged before it made its way up the wide chimney. Each flame seemed to the man who gazed into the fire to nod a nod of recognition, and to speak with a voice meant for his ear alone.

'It is a grand thing,' he thought, 'to have imagination in small things as in great . . . .

'And now that I have an established position, and an audience secured to me, I shall revolutionise history. Nobody—I am not wrong—*nobody* has understood how history ought to be written or to be taught. Carlyle'* (he called him 'Car-r-lyle') 'had visions of it—he was a Scot, too—but he was too erratic. Michelet* had fine ideas, but he was radically unsound. But with learning *and* imagination . . . .

'A bit of ship's wood now.' As he spoke, a flame of exquisite turquoise shot out of the log. 'A mere bit of ship's wood.'

And the Professor beheld a wonderful procession marching before the eye of his mind. He saw vast rivers—so large that the Thames and the Seine and the Rhine were no better than small tributary streams to them. On these great waters were sailing what seemed at first but logs of wood. A second view showed them to be hollowed in the centre; and hairy, skin-clad men and women were inside them, bent low, manœuvring uncouth paddles.

Then, with a swift turn of thought, he saw a great battle going on hard by where is now the Port of Suez. Arrows were flying through the air. The ships were level in the centre, with high stems and sterns, and square-rigged. How heavy hung those sails in the scorching air! On some of the ships fought black Lybians, their shaggy locks bound with fillets of gold. There were red Egyptians naked to the loins, girt with white cloths, and blue and green beads in their hair. There were hardy, wild-looking Siculi, and Achæans who had collars of gold and silver . . . .

Nay, behold! these ships all passed out of sight, and there was to be seen but a single merchant galley, and it was navigating in a cold sea, hung round with fog. The sailors shuddered as they plied the oar or trimmed the sail, and told each other dreadful stories of the land of the Cimmerians, whither they were bound. Only one keen-eyed Greek stood at the prow, and would not turn back. Now, lo! the foggy sea was full of floating things! Were they jelly-fish? But how hard and how bitter cold!

A sluggish sea, and almost stagnant, which we may believe girds in and encloses the whole world. For here the light of the setting sun lingers on till sunrise, bright enough to dim the light of the stars. More than that, it is asserted that the sound of his rising is to be heard, and the form of the God and the glory round his head may be seen. Only thus far, and here rumour seems truth, does the world extend.

Yet now out of this same brumous sea came a shout. And behold, one after another advanced from out of the mist the long-boats, the dragon ships of the Northmen, spinning under the sweeping oars. Their sails were square, and of many colours—some blue, some yellow, some red. The gunwales were low in the water; round shields hung about them.

A sea-ward from the low misty land has sighted them. He is the Scylding's warden, and he holds sea-ward there at earth's end that no foe may come into the Danish land. Now he calls out to the approaching keels:—

'What arm-bearing men be ye, in byrnies clad, who thus come in your foaming keels over the water-ways, over the sea-deeps hither?'

And they answer—nay, I know not what, for this vision, too, faded away. The sea logs sent up now only yellow flames, which coloured the dense smoke which hung over them. And a new and unbidden image now rose out of the smother. It was the face of a young girl—golden-haired and tender-eyed; more beautiful to behold, even than superb Egyptians or stately Greeks, or the all-conquering men of the North. So thought the Professor likewise.

The gentle eyes lifted their soft lids and looked straight into the eyes of the man and smiled a recognition. And the mouth—or was it only the eyes that spoke?—uttered a single word.

'Choose,' said the girl.

And the Professor chose.

The face was gone. The flames whispered a little while, asking what the unbidden image could mean. Then they stopped whispering. The smoke ceased mounting up the wide chimney. The ashes glowed for a time; till their glow left them, and with gentle patterings they fell cold into the cold grate.

But the Professor was colder still.

VI—BLAUBEUREN

At Blaubeuren, in Swabia, is the deepest pool in the world; so profound that no one has yet sounded the bottom of it. And it is also the bluest water to be met with anywhere; so blue that it rivals the deepest colour of the summer sky.

What wonder, therefore, that the reflection of Vega, that bright star, should have mistaken the element in which it found itself, and have supposed that this blue was really the infinite blue of heaven; and, by consequence, that itself was not a reflection at all, but one of the shining orbs of the firmament.

'How,' it said to itself, looking at Vega, 'that fellow looks up at me from below! How he envies me the immeasurable height at which I am placed, and my eternal circuit through the ether.'

And in these thoughts it floated serenely on through the unfathomable azure deep.

But when ten minutes had gone by, Vega, looking towards the earth, saw only the slumbering pine-woods of the Vosges, and no longer looked at its reflection in the well of Blaubeuren.

And the reflection of Vega, which had supposed itself a star, had not yet discovered that it was not one, for it was non-existent.

VII—THE LOVER

She ceased speaking, and Hope, which up to that moment had stood at his side, spread wide her wings, and, without a cry, leapt into the air. In a minute more she had diminished to a speck, and the next moment was gone.

Then he heard loud discordant laughter in his ears, like the laughter of fiends, and knew that he was falling through space. The mocking laughs seemed to rain down upon him, as pebbles might rain down upon one descending a mine. But his fall was far deeper. For through the centuries he fell ever down and down, with no vision of the place where he must strike the ground, to his instant destruction; nor yet with any power to gaze upward; not even toward the demon shapes who were watching from above, and of whom the laughter still pattered down upon his head.

Then behold, his fall was ended! But in lieu of striking upon the bottom of the abyss, he found that wings had grown upon him during the years of his descent, and he could fly. With some sense of power, some hope of liberty, he stretched those wings.

But ah! It was only in a brown subterraneous world that he could move onward. For ever did he beat his wings and continued his low flight in the same brown world where nothing was visible except a kind of dim shadows of the things he had known and cared for in that other life. So girt round with twilight and dun shapes he journeyed on and on in level flight.

Meanwhile, the minute hand upon his watch had made three jerks.

VIII—THE MANIKINS

'O Maro! What island is that which lies thus beautifully suspense between the opal water and the pearly sky?'

'We are making for it,' answered my guide.

Indeed, we bent our course straight thither. As much it resembles flying, I deem, as sailing the passing over that element which in Limbo they call 'the sea.'

'How like to England it is after all,' I sighed. (However great may be your love of travel, you love it less when there can be no travelling back.) Umbrageous, grass-grown was the land which momentarily rose clearer from its silver setting; full of shadowy oaks and lordly elms. I heard a lark carolling, and caught the distant clangour of church bells. Yet there were foreign growths mingling with these homely ones, from, it seemed to me, all parts of the world. Eucalyptus I saw, and palms. On one hand a Wellingtonia Gigantea* pointed to the skies.

And now we landed. It was another home. The islanders spoke English, save a certain proportion who talked in Scottish of a kind I could not understand. Was it not a new and better England? The men I thought were taller, more manly, braver, purer than I had seen them elsewhere; the women nobler, truer, more beautiful. 'I shall soon get to know and love these people,' I said to myself, 'for see with what a companion I come hither. The greater these are, the more will they reverence this Puissant Shade: and me for his sake they will cherish.'

I own it was no small delight to me to find that in this world poverty and its deformities hardly were. I caught scarce a glimpse of rags and dirt. Vulgar toil, too, had hid itself away. Maybe I was a thought amazed to find the doings of these men and women so much like the doings of the leisured class down below. The men shot, fished, rode, played the games of golf and tennis. The women shopped and danced and gossiped and drank tea of the afternoon; though of reason all these things took a larger meaning in that diviner air, among a higher type of English men and women.

They were not proud, neither, but seemed to invite me to be of their company. Of the men many had the look and bearing of officers and gentlemen. I was introduced to one young fellow called, as I think, 'Little Freddy,' who seemed to be a favourite with all, as indeed he had a taking open countenance, candour and innocence personified, one might have said.

I did not therefore need the countenance of my guide. But I confess my first surprise came from discovering how few there seemed to have had previous acquaintance with him. All spoke of him with reverence when I whispered who my companion was. But if I may use the phrase, they rather shuffled away from a personal introduction.

'Is it indeed Maro?' they would say with no small unction. 'Ah, ah,' and no more did I get from them than that. Perhaps one would go on to ask me if we had not once met at Lady Betty Bessborough's, or some such matter.

The Master on his side stood apart and seemed to have no greater wish to mingle with these groups than they had to see him among them. And for a brief space this seemed to me almost pitiful in him. I longed to bring about an approach 'twixt him and them.

Full of these thoughts I turned and caught in his eye a smile which were I speaking of one less mighty I should call quizzical. At first I could not but muse what this should mean. At first only: very soon I understood it well enough. . . . . .

My Mighty Guide approached me. 'And now,' said he, 'I must leave you here, and glad am I that I quit you while in such brave company.'

'Do not go! O! for the great God's sake do not leave me here,' I cried.

'What, what is it?' he answered, still with that set smile. 'An hour ago you thought that I . . . .' And while he spoke he was still moving as if to depart.

I could not let him finish. 'Twas a thing too serious, too horrible.

'You know what it is,' I replied, my eyes starting, my hair bristling on the crown of my head. 'You know what it is' (my voice shook). 'They, they are *not alive*. They are but dummies, manikins, with a semblance of vitality. Things ingeniously contrived by some cunning mechanician to go through the postures of men and women, and deceive me for one short hour. O! I cannot live with such as these!'

And I turned my eyes to where, on the lawn hard by, a very gallant-looking colonel, excellently dressed, was talking to two charming-looking women. 'Every moment that I continue to look at them fills me with fresh terror.' And in my fear I caught hold of the mantle of the Shade. Whereupon the expression of his face changed, and very kindly and gently he sought to comfort me.

'You are indeed more unhappy or happier than most,' he said, 'in that you have found out so quickly the mechanic contrivance by which these islanders here are made. Many have spent days and months, nay years with them blindly content. But now I tell you this for your comfort. These beings, who fill you with so much terror, are not the only indwellers of the land. If you can win your way through them you will come to another race who live apart, and hold not like these easy commerce with the first-come. You have read of those other men and women. I deem it unlucky to pronounce their names here: for the names are ever taken in vain—as mine is. Of the beings themselves these of the outer zone know as much as you have seen they know of me. Therefore take this only from me, that of a surety, if thou penetrate farther from the coast thou shalt find the Colonel and his son and his niece; thou shalt find the Foundling and the Vicar and the Uncle and all the rest of the goodly society who have planted and watered in this island and made the land what it is.'

And therewith the August Shadow beckoned thrice with his hand as if to urge me forward. And when I looked again he was gone.

IX—The Black Mass

One, two, three, four, five, six, seven, eight, nine, ten, eleven, twelve, more and more. Why did the clock-bell keep on striking?

But, ah! why did the moon, the gibbous moon which I had just seen set behind the towers of the Trocadero, begin to rise again from the west? Who else has ever seen a moon rise slowly from the west? Would I had never seen it nor the shadows that it threw!

Without doubt the front of Notre Dame, before which I stood, was wondrously lit up by its beams. All the shadows behind its countless images, its pinnacles, its gargoyles, frets, and capitals were not black but blue: yea, and they moved and flickered like little blue flames. So strange a sight I never beheld. More, it was impossible to say that the solid stonework itself was steady and not rather like some vast and noiseless beacon-fire flickering and changing in its bright white flames and its blue; once on a while the white and blue would be shot with streaks of yellow and of red. I looked spell-bound and could not turn my head away.

When I did at last a sea of blackness seemed to lie all round: the sky itself was reft of light. Yet was this blackness not so black but that it had ruddy gleams. Nor was it steady any more than the bright pile before my face. It, too, seemed to pulse as pulses the smoke of a fire. And the blackest blackness of all was moving towards me.

Yes, because there were—what? People coming out of the shadow. Yea, indeed, shapes of men moving on to the front to where I stood. A mighty company, and my eyes, better used now to the exchange of light and dark, recognised them: these were men and women whom I had seen somewhere before.

That old woman with a wisp of grey hair alongside her parchment face, her jaw fallen side-wise in a fashion that had a hint of comedy mingling with its infinite terror. There was the man with blotchy nose, his glassy eyes still looking stupidly at one as though through his cups he had slipped into a sounder sleep; the thin-faced girl: she alone had the true look of despair upon her face; the toothless old man who had just a streak of black blood behind his black lips. I had seen all these before. They were crowding up from the back of the church: from whence?

From the Morgue. It was there I had seen those who headed the march. First came the newest dead: then followed troops upon troops of earlier victims. I had indeed happened upon the night of the Black Mass. The late-comers made me the sign and I was obliged to enter the church.

The church was dark. What wailing sound was that as of the wind through the masts and the rotting cordage of innumerable wrecks? Was I indeed within the church or out upon some barren marsh hard by the sea? Was that moaning the voice of the organ only? What demon was it who touched the stops?

More unearthly still when the organ ceased its prelude and the chant began. All men joined in it, with wide speculativeless eyes and wider jaws, jaws fallen all apart, now to this side, now to that.

'Exurge, Domine,'* I heard, 'Salvum me fac, Satanas.'* Though their eyes looked no whither and their mouths could not shut they sang deafeningly loud. And there were such crowds and crowds of them. I thought I had entered only at the very end of the church. Now, there were blue faces and fallen jaws before me, behind, on every side. It was too dark to see how far they extended.

'O, how shall I ever escape,' I thought, and my tongue clove to my lips; when turning round I saw one dead who was looking at me. He made me the sign to go on and sing with the rest.

At last the dreadful chant was over. A cowled priest mounted the pulpit stairs. Him I could see plainly while all else was so dim. Perhaps he carried a light. That which he held in his hand—a lantern?—no, now I saw it was an hour-glass, but the sands in it were glowing with heat. How he bent as if he bore some load! The light from the hour-glass flashed upon something over his shoulder, and when he straighted himself in the pulpit I heard a clang as of steel. But still his cowl was down, the red light glowing thereon left only a black hole where his face was. Then at last he threw back his cowl and there was a murmur as if of applause all through the vast church, a sighing murmur and a rattle as of jaws loosely meeting. Nor was I surprised to see at length the face of the preacher—that it was Old Death himself.

How could either surprise or terror be any greater with me than they were now? How the fellow grinned and nodded over the pulpit-cushion! Yet, had I known what was to follow I could have wished that sermon to go on for ever.

They had already begun to hand the basket down the church. Yes, in the dimness, as of a man looking out over a moonlit landscape, I could see hands stretched out, the bread distributed, the *pain beni*.* The basket-edge shone white in the dim moonlight. But it is black bread that they have got inside. Truly a black mass. It was coming nearer and nearer, the fatal basket. Ugh! Was it *bread* at all that it contained? Ah, no; my nose told me what it was.

'And you must eat of it,' cried at that moment a voice behind me.

'It is flesh of our flesh, flesh of the Morgue; flesh of the girl who has been betrayed to ruin, of the man who has been ground down to drink and death. Of that you too shall be.'

'Christ save us!'

It broke the spell. I was no longer rooted to the spot. I turned to rush from the church.

Whereupon a death-like yell rose from all that vast multitude. Hands were held out to stop me. But I saw that the owners of them were sightless.

Yet the sound of that great cry went on reverberating in my head, and it echoes still.

X—THE SKELETONS

I opine that it was in Surrey, because of the character of the scenery which is indelibly impressed on my memory, as you may suppose when you hear the sequel. An endless road, hard, straight, well-made, stretched between a border of dark fir trees. To what distance on either side the road the fir-wood extended I knew not; for I walked but little. My uncles seldom or never went for walks; and I had no other companions save them and my dog, Plato. The one object which my uncles held up before themselves and me in those earliest days was the getting rid of Time and Space. Geography, therefore, was not a subject to be encouraged; and that is why I do not know to this day what part of England (supposing it to have been England) we lived in. What I remember and shall ever remember is the straight white wood sloping for a long way (an endless way it seemed when I was very young) up hill. When you had reached the top of the slope you gazed over a very considerable country, thickly wooded still chiefly by firs; and a long way off traces of human habitations, brown hamlets and dim-discovered spires. Just at this point, the top of the slope, our long white road was joined by another, which was divided into two branches, thereby enclosing a triangular patch of fir-wood, small, but very thickly planted, so that save on an exceptionally bright day you could scarcely see into the middle of it.

There was a tragic history connected with this little triangular patch of fir: though that has nothing to do with *my* history. Years ago two of my uncles, Simon and Caspar, had been
walking along by that copse and noticed an evil smell. Their
noses led them to penetrate the thicket, and in the very centre
they found two bodies, both showing marks of violence, but
now evidently dead some days and much decomposed. They
were the bodies of two brothers. The dark story connected
with their death had never been fully told me. It hinted, as I
now understand, at an unholy love between a brother and
sister, and the punishment therefor at the hands of the other
brother, who, after he had killed the offender, committed
suicide. Wherefore the triangular patch of wood was always
a haunted spot to me. Even in the brightest sunshine I grew
cold as I reached the summit of the long slope, and my appre-
ciation of the wide champaign which lay beyond was always
dimmed by the uneasy feeling which made me from time to
time glance sideways at the dark thicket. To have advanced
farther still and have left that thicket *between* me and home
was beyond my courage in those days. And I must have gone
alone; for nowadays none of my uncles ever adventured so far,
until——

My uncles. I called each of them 'uncle' alike; though to
which I was really related, or whether I were actually related
by blood to any, I am in some doubt. Uncle Simon, Uncle
Caspar, Uncle Melchior, Uncle Balthasar: thus were they
called. Curious names for English old bachelors, which is what
I take them to have been. Each lived in his separate cottage,
two on one side of the road, two on the other. All the four
cottages stood a little back from the road and among the fir
trees; but not all at equal distances from it. No one was visible from any of the others. These four cottages were the only
dwelling-places with which I had a near acquaintance. I myself
belonged to all or none of them; might sleep in any one that I
chose, but never in a quite properly constituted bed; on a sofa
in the sitting-room in one; in another, on a settee; in a third,

in a shakedown in an alcove, just behind the kitchen chimney, while in the kitchen itself the old housekeeper snored. She 'did for' all my uncles. They dined by rotation in the four parlours of the four cottages—their only living rooms.

If my daylight reminiscences are connected mostly with the long white road and some portions of the fir-wood on either side, my evening visions are of one or another of these four cottage parlours, and of my uncles, after supper had been cleared away, sitting round the square table covered with its checked table-cloth, reading aloud and arguing. One candle for the reader and no more. The candle threw huge shadows of my uncles' four heads upon the four walls, made deep lines under their eyes, or illuminated the under portions of their faces only, when as rarely they raised their chins to laugh, and threw their foreheads into shade.

I must have had a wonderful memory, for I carried away whole conversations without comprehending a word of them. 'Time' and 'Space' figured much in their argumentations, 'Subjectivity,' 'Objectivity,' 'Reason,' and 'Understanding,' the 'Categories.' Then there was much of 'Causality' and the 'Categorical Imperative,' along with a many other things, with whose names, reft of all meaning to me, I got familiar enough. At last I began to attach some idea of my own finding to this jargon of names and terms. For instance, as I saw Uncle Caspar—of the grey hair and mild blue eyes—often passing a hand now down one side of his head now down another, I settled it in my own mind that one grey tuft was 'Time,' the other 'Space,' and that he was smoothing them out of existence in that fashion. As between Reason and Understanding, Caspar and Balthasar were for my imagination on the side of the first, Simon and Melchior—bald-headed Uncle Melchior—the partisans of the second. Simon would represent the 'Ultimate Truth in Being,' Melchior the 'Ultimate Truth in Causation,' Balthasar the 'Ultimate Truth in Knowledge,' or 'Logic,' Caspar the 'Ultimate Truth in Action,' or 'Ethic.' What these phrases meant I know now as well as I did then; that is to say, not at all. But that I use them rightly, in so far as my uncles did so, I have no sort of doubt.

Then came the change. It followed, I believe, the importation of some fresh books into the colony; or perhaps I only guess this from my later knowledge of things. But I know that quite a new set of words began to pass from mouth to mouth about the square tables and across the checked table-cloths. Now the talk was first of the difference between 'Vivid and Faint Ideas,' between 'Reality' and 'Dreams.' There was much of 'the continued redistribution of matter and motion.' Then such words as 'Nerve Ganglions,' 'Protein Substance,' 'Protein Threads,' 'Granular Protoplasm,' never heard among us before, began to make their appearance. And from that time 'Ultimate Truth,' 'Reason,' 'Understanding,' and the old set of phrases were heard no more. I was not now told to get rid of notions of Time and Space. But, if I hinted at an *intention* of going to walk with Plato along the road, my uncles would shake their heads sadly, and intimate that this word 'intention' had no 'correlation in reality,' and that if a certain molecular change took place in my brain, I should go out; if it did not take place, I should stay at home. They themselves went out less and less, and indeed seemed to exert themselves in every way less and less. In consequence they lost their appetites and grew visibly thinner. But if I said, 'It is because you never come out of doors,' they only smiled still more pityingly, and intimated that they were waiting for the 'molecular changes' that would *send* them out of doors without their going through the pretence of intending to go.

And when they talked it was still of reality that they spoke; and when they were silent—and now they sat silent for long spells—it seemed to be for reality that they were waiting, waiting. They cared less and less about their food; and, what was worse for their nephew, they extended their indifference from themselves to him. So that I often grew faint after my walks. For in spite of their dissent, or of their tacit disapproval, my dog Plato continued to tempt me to come out with him.

Wherever we went now, into the wood or along the road, we two went alone. One day, faint from my meagre diet, I fell down in the roadway before I could get home again.

What happened after that I scarcely know. I have an impression of being taken up by a man whom I instinctively called 'the Tinker'; but why I gave him that name I cannot tell. All my sensations were so faint that I now realised fully, and for the first time, what my uncles had meant by their 'vivid' and 'faint' impressions. And from what I had gathered of their talk, I was, I knew, to regard these faint impressions as having no reality, as being no better than a dream. It was, therefore, in a dream that the *Tinker* (why 'the Tinker,' I wonder still) carried me off in his cart bowling along that great white road, that he gave me food, that I slept; that I was conscious of bowling along the white road once more. That the Tinker set me down again and said: '*Now* go and find your uncles,' and then went on, a black patch he and his cart and the shadow of his cart, growing smaller and smaller as they passed toward the brow of the hill.

I stood up. It was moonlight. Strange that I had not perceived it before. That, then, was why the Tinker and his cart looked so black upon the road. And, yes! this must be almost the very place I had fallen down upon, and here was Plato come up to lick my hand. And now I had turned into the path which led to Uncle Caspar's house, and then from Uncle Caspar's to Uncle Balthasar's.

I had passed the first house—for it was empty—and got in sight of the second. As I did this, its door opened, and there came out—four skeletons. But in each skeleton I recognised a something familiar, which made me at once know them for my Uncles Simon, Caspar, Melchior, Balthasar. This one had Caspar's slight stoop, that had Melchior's habit of placing his hands upon his hips, and that third still cracked his bony finger-joints as Uncle Simon did. Out they all four came—they did not see me—arm-in-arm, and marched in a long swinging step the score of yards or so which separated the house from the road. And when there, they all, as if in time, struck the bones of their feet against the hard road. 'Ah, that's solid, there's something real in that,' they said or croaked as the bones rattled. 'Ganglions, nerve-centres? That, too, was all a set of rubbish, resolving itself, if you went far enough, to *motion* and *heat*, and I don't know what not. But bones. There's something solid in bones when all's done. Bones, bones. There's something solid in bones.'

It came out in a clattering, gurgling sound, and yet with a sort of tune as if in a chorus, 'Bones, bones. There's something solid in bones,' while their feet struck the ground in time as if they were dancing. And I could not choose but follow them. Thus we all passed on: these four in front and I behind. And still they went on, on, up the long white road, bathed in the moonlight; and still their feet beat a rattling time, and still they clattered and gurgled 'Bones, bones. There's something solid in bones'; until we reached the summit of the slope where the cross-road came, and where stood the dark triangular copse, now black as night. Then a sudden fear seized me and loosened the joints of my knees so that I could not go on. But I still watched them as they slowly dipped down over the brow of the hill; and I still heard them rattling and clattering, 'Bones, bones. There's something solid in bones.'

NOTES

Entre Chien et Loup

x   *frore*: frozen or frosty.

The Message from the God

3   *temenos*: a sacred grove.

4   *Marcomanni*: a Germanic tribe, fought against by the emperor
      Marcus Aurelius in the second century A.D.
      Gryneian Apollo: Grynion (or Gryna, or Grynus), a town in Asia
      Minor, had a temple dedicated to Apollo, which also functioned
      as an oracle.

8   *lemures*: in Roman mythology, *lemures* were vengeful and malig-
      nant spirits of the restless dead.
      coloni: tenant farmers.

Elizabeth

10   *epigraph*: from *Oedipus at Colonus* by Sophocles. Likely Keary's
      own translation. (Cf. Gilbert Murray: 'What is the grove? And
      what God haunteth it? Untouched it is, untrod. Dread Virgins
      hold Their court here, born of Earth and Darkness old.')

12   *kine*: archaic plural of cow.

19   *screech-owl*: here, the archaic name of the barn owl, rather than
      the New World screech owl.

23   *ban*: in this context, an ecclesiastical denunciation or anathema-
      tization.
      gospel-oak: According to J. G. Strutt in *Sylva Britannica* (1830),
      gospel-oaks were markers of parish boundaries. In an annual
      ritual before Holy Thursday, the village priest would recite
      passages from the Gospels at specific trees. This served to both
      bless the parish and also to transfer knowledge of the parish
      limits across generations. Strutt suggests the ritual has its basis

in the pagan feast of Terminalia, which served a similar func-
tion. Keary's use here reinforces the idea that village in the
story is an outlier, on the edge of the unknown forest.

24   *beldame*: a grandmother or, pejoratively, a witch or hag.
25   *sooth*: truth.
     bailey: more usually rendered 'bailie' in this archaic variant of
     bailiff, or district officer.
30   *hist*: an archaic exclamation used to attract attention or enjoin
     silence.
31   *doles*: alms, the distribution of charity.
33   *baldaquin*: richly-embroidered brocade.
40   *recked*: noticed.
47   *pyx*: a box containing the consecrated bread of the Eucharist.

The Four Students

52   *truckle-beds*: low beds, moveable on castors (truckles).
54   *Ja, Pa, Asmodai, Aleph, Beleph, Adonai, Gormo, Mormo, Sadaï, Gal-
     zael, Asrael, Tangon, Mangon, Porphrael!*: a doggerel approxima-
     tion of the litanies of demonic names typical of books of black
     magic. It is a combination of words invented by Keary and
     those drawn from various mythological sources. The phrase
     'Gormo, Mormo' is reminiscent of H. P. Lovecraft's 'Gorgo,
     Mormo, Thousand-face moon' formulation in 'The Horror of
     Red Hook' (1927). It is conceivable that Lovecraft could have
     encountered Keary's story, which was published in the U.S. in
     the *Eclectic Magazine* in 1892.
58   *chouan*: old French for the tawny owl.
61   *métayers*: agricultural labourers engaged in return for a propor-
     tion of the produce; sharecroppers.
64   *Carmagnole*: *La Carmagnole* was a revolutionary song, with an
     accompanying wild dance, said to be of Piedmontese origin. It
     is also mentioned by Dickens in *A Tale of Two Cities* (1859).
66   *sabots*: wooden clogs, associated with the lower classes.
     ci-devant: nobility refusing to acknowledge the post-revolution-
     ary social system (literally 'from before').
70   *fillet*: a circlet or headband.
79   *Thermidor*: the eleventh month in the Republican calendar. 9
     Thermidor Year II (27 July 1794) saw the downfall of Robespierre
     and the end of the Reign of Terror.

PHANTASIES

82   *atelier*: an *atelier* is an artist's workshop or studio.
      tablier: apron.
84   *façon de parler*: manner of speaking.
85   *espiègle*: impish or mischievous.
87   *Père La Chaise*: François de La Chaise (1624-1709), was father
      confessor to King Louis XIV of France. Named after him, Père
      Lachaise Cemetery remains the largest in the city of Paris.
92   *Carlyle*: Thomas Carlyle (1795-1881), the Scottish historian and
      essayist.
      Michelet: Jules Michelet (1798-1874), the French historian.
96   *Wellingtonia Gigantea*: the giant sequoia, or giant redwood.
100   *Exurge, Domine*: Latin: 'Arise O Lord.'
      Salvum me fac, Satanas: Latin: 'Save me, Satan.'
101   *pain beni*: consecrated bread.